"I'm through," Peter said. "I'm going away where my father will never find me."

"Why, Peter? What has he done?" Dolores asked.

"He's burned the verses, the sketches, the notes for my play—everything I've written. And he says I'm not to waste my time with that stuff anymore. He might as well tell me not to breathe!"

"But where can you go? What can you do?"

"I'll get a job. I have some money and can sell the car. It's mine. I bought it myself. I'll go to New York."

"But you'll be leaving me," she said in a low voice. "You can't, Peter. Take me with you. You'll work and I'll work too. You needn't feel the least obligation toward me. You'll just love me . . . and be free. We'll never be like other people, married people who grow tired and restless and hate each other. We'll be ourselves. You and I. It will be wonderful!"

D1247482

Books by Faith Baldwin

Garden Oats	*Private Duty*
The Incredible Year	*Innocent Bystander*
Arizona Star	*Sleeping Beauty*
The West Wind	*The Heart Remembers*
One More Time	*Alimony*
Medical Center	*A Job for Jenny*
The Lonely Man	*And New Stars Burn*
He Married a Doctor	*That Man Is Mine*
Love's a Puzzle	*Give Love the Air*
Honor Bound	*Twenty-four Hours a Day*
Career by Proxy	*Look Out for Liza*
Station Wagon Set	*Thresholds*
The Heart Has Wings	*Blue Horizons*
A Close and Quiet Love	*Enchanted Oasis*
Temporary Address: Reno	*The Rest of My Life With You*
The Three Faces of Love	*Beauty*
Letty and the Law	*Rehearsal for Love*
The Moon's Our Home	*Make-Believe*
The Golden Shoestring	*No Private Heaven*
White Magic	*Change of Heart*
You Can't Escape	*"Something Special"*
Yesterday's Love	*Take What You Want*
Three Women	

Published By
WARNER BOOKS

ARE THERE WARNER BOOKS
YOU WANT BUT CANNOT FIND IN YOUR LOCAL STORES?

You can get any Warner Books title in print. Simply send title and retail price, plus 35¢ to cover mailing and handling costs for each book desired. New York State residents add applicable sales tax. Enclose check or money order only, no cash please, to:

WARNER BOOKS
P.O. BOX 690
NEW YORK, N.Y. 10019

GARDEN OATS

by
Faith Baldwin

WARNER BOOKS

A Warner Communications Company

WARNER BOOKS EDITION

Copyright 1929, 1931 by Faith Baldwin Cuthrell
Copyright renewed © 1957 by Faith Baldwin Cuthrell
All rights reserved

ISBN 0-446-86267-3

This Warner Books Edition is published by
arrangement with Holt, Rinehart and Winston

Cover art by Elaine Duilla

Warner Books, Inc., 75 Rockefeller Plaza, New York, N.Y. 10019

Ⓦ A Warner Communications Company

Printed in Canada.

Not associated with Warner Press, Inc. of Anderson, Indiana

10 9 8 7 6 5 4 3 2 1

In admiration and in gratitude to Judge Ben B. Lindsey whose actual experience suggested the theme of this story and whose gracious cooperation permitted it to be written

CHAPTER I

THE pale penetration of early spring sunlight pierced the wavering veils of fog drifting over the town, and invaded the window where Dolores stood, fingering a sash-cord, her mouth drooping with discontent.

The drawing-room glimmered wanly as a ghost. Faint shining from crystal lusters pendant from girandoles was like a memory of light. The white-paneled walls, the faded blue brocade, and the slim gilt chairs were touched to a dim color. A French window stood open to the garden and the fragrance of narcissus and hyacinth crept in, laced with the bitter virile scent of salt.

In the quiet room where all things drowsed, where tradition and legend, unalterable, moved like shadows, Dolores Brewster was as challenging as the note of a silver trumpet, as glowing as roses in midsummer, as rebel as autumnal winds. Tall, slim, deep-breasted, she stood motionless, her exotic, oval face sullen with the burden of unsatisfied youth. Above the mantelpiece the portrait of the first Dolores, the Spanish girl who had married a Yankee sea-captain and beaten her bright wings vainly against the walls of this old New England house, smiled down upon her great-granddaughter, her eyes brilliant under a black mantilla, her slim hand coquetting with a painted fan.

From this Dolores, dust in a quiet churchyard, the seventeen year old girl dreaming rebelliously by the window inherited her great eyes, and her red mouth, and her

7

ivory pallor; from her, too, the arched, narrow feet, the long hands stretching out for life.

She was as alien in the square brick house on Pleasant Street as her great-grandmother had been. She was a flame in a cool garden, and a gypsy song in a cloister. "A throwback," her cousin Carolyn would murmur regretfully, marking how the most simple and conservative linen frock shaped to the girl's superb young figure; how her amazing beauty dominated the quiet colors chosen for her.

Cousin Carolyn and her widowed sister Sarah heard, occasionally, of the manners and morals of the new generation. They were disturbed, and appalled, but these tales were but echoes from another world. As their mother and grandmother had lived, they lived. Dolores was their charge and their delight. She had come to them as a baby, to the old house in which her people had been born and which had passed from her branch of the family in her grandfather's time, and which would one day return to her, the last of her race. Carolyn and Sarah were elderly then, and had been panic-stricken at this altering of the even tenor of their ways. But they had accepted their duty, and had even loved it. So they had brought up Dolores, as they themselves had been brought up, sheltered as a nun.

Dolores had left the small private school in the town the preceding Autumn. Her cousins had been horrified at her demand for college. Women of their race and class did not attend universities. They left learning to the men. Carolyn and Sarah had met a few college girls in their occasional excursions into the shifting society of summer visitors. These girls had been masculine, loud voiced; they had worn their skirts too short; some of them painted their faces . . . one had smoked at tea in Mrs. Lacy's drawing room.

Dolores turned from the window as Carolyn Brewster came lightly into the room, walking with that grace of carriage which is given only to dignity and breeding.

"Have you been out, Dolores? We were looking for you. Mrs. Evans has gone. She wished you to try on the gray chiffon."

"I walked," Dolores answered in her voice that was like

rough velvet, "I couldn't stay in the house. I went down to the bridge . . . in the fog. . . ."

"I see. Sarah will be down directly. It must be tea time."

Miss Brewster sat down on a teakwood chair, her back erect, her feet crossed before her on a mahogany footstool. She was thin and shapeless in the black she had worn for many years. Her blue eyes were undimmed behind the old-fashioned spectacles, her face exquisitely lined, her narrow mouth a faint pink. She opened a sewing table and drew out a piece of her interminable embroidery, fitted a thimble, and sorted pastel colored silks. As she moved heavy gold and onyx earrings swung from pierced ears to the color of faintly yellowed wax.

She glanced at Dolores. The girl was very still. She had that rare quality of stillness which suggests vivid motion—flashing life held in leash. Her cousin asked, gently:

"Will you tell Letty that we are ready?"

Dolores moved across the room with a controlled grace that had something burning and checked about it. One felt she wished to run.

When she returned she found her Cousin Sarah there, turning over the pages of a magazine. Sarah Clifford was younger than her sister, plumper, more colorful, with bright eyes and a small, full mouth, sunken at the corners. She possessed an air of arrested youth, of a Valentine's Day sentimentality, and she regarded her spinster sister with a faint, pitying superiority—that of the adult toward the child—as if her brief married life had invested her with a sort of perpetual claim to leadership.

"Play for us," she bade Dolores in her rather deep voice, and Dolores sat down at the piano and bent her head—heavy with its weight of blue-black hair—over the yellowing keys. She played well, she had good teachers. But she alarmed them by her adventuring into a world of wilder music than they had ever dreamed of. Through the restrained, adequate technique they taught her, her temperament broke, passionate and desirous, hungering after life.

Now she made quiet music in the hushed room. Carolyn

9

nodded over the pale roses of her embroidering, and Sarah sat silent, thinking back, her austerely romantic heart reflecting the memory of a lost love time that had been fleet and yet survived—scented with lavender and lighted by impossible moonlight.

Letty brought in the tea things, and presently Miss Carolyn was pouring the amber of China tea from a squat Paul Revere pot into the Lowestoft cups.

I hate tea, thought Dolores suddenly, setting down her cup with a miniature crash which startled her cousins. She reached for a sandwich—cut finger-thin and spread with beach plum jam—and bit into it with her strong white teeth.

Her cousins were talking gently, of church matters; of someone's new baby; of an impending marriage in the Lacy family. Now Sarah turned to Dolores and asked, with an archness that belonged in a Godey print:

"Have you heard from dear Peter lately?"

The question was superfluous. Sarah showed no astonishment as Dolores shook her head. The cousins knew when the letters came with the Cambridge postmark; that they did not demand to read them was a fairly recent concession to Dolores' "age."

"Such a nice boy," commented Miss Carolyn, inevitably, looking for the sugar tongs. "It doesn't seem possible that he is in his second year at the University. It seems so short a time ago that he first came here to visit his mother's people, a curly-headed lad in petticoats."

Dolores laughed. The sound was like a gleam of gold and a flash of scarlet in the dim room.

"Not petticoats, surely, Cousin Carolyn!"

"My brothers wore them until they were six,"—Miss Carolyn defended herself—"white with blue sashes. . . ."

Sarah laughed too, comfortably.

"But Peter is of another generation. I remember him quite well. Knickerbockers—generally torn—his hands in his pockets and his head on one side, begging for another cookie. He always liked Martha's cookies."

"He does yet," said Dolores, with a faint chuckle. She was thinking . . . I must tell Peter about the petticoats.

10

. . . She was always thinking . . . *I must tell Peter.* . . .
He was all she had, mind and heart had opened to him
as naturally as a flower to the drawing sun ever since they
were children exploring the town, sitting on the bridge—
their legs dangling—climbing the pear tree in the garden,
and getting roundly scolded for their adventure. But what
an adventure it had been, that first time, a tall tree reaching to heaven, green leaves all about them, blossoms falling, and a blue sky. . . .

She began to count the days before Peter would come
home for his Easter vacation. He would drive over from
the mill town where he lived with his father in that great
gloomy house, and they would walk, and laugh, and talk.
. . . She had so much to tell him. They would quarrel over
some of the books he had sent her this past winter—great
books with long titles, little books with frothy chapter
headings, slim books with poetry caught between their
pages. She had grown clever at concealing some of the
books from her cousins. They wouldn't understand. They
had been dead for such a long time—she thought—moving ghostlike through a world of their own, not realizing
that Time had gone on without them; that all around them
things were changing; old standards being discarded; old
institutions coming upon the dissecting tables of the
modern thinkers.

Now she smiled, aloofly, and thought of . . . Peter in
petticoats.

Her cousins looked at one another, and Sarah nodded,
smiling. They approved of Peter Comstock. He had background and breeding, and charming manners. He had the
fearless look of race and dignity. They liked him. He did
not chatter, nor was he slangy. He was quiet and defer-
ential, deft with a cushion, a teacup or a footstool. They
disliked young men who talked too much. A gentleman
had no need to exploit himself in speech.

Peter's mother had been born in this very town, not far
from the house on Pleasant Street. Marrying, she had
moved to a nearby city and there had died. Her husband
was a substantial, good man, and a pillar of the church.
His cotton mills dominated the city in which he was the

11

outstanding figure, as his father had been before him. Peter was heir to more than breeding. But the sisters never spoke openly to each other of their plans for the young people. It would have been indelicate.

Now Dolores left them and went to her own room and sat down at her rosewood desk to write to Peter. The open windows overlooked Pleasant Street and its double row of elms and chestnuts. A cool wind blew in and ruffled the curtains. The room was white and mahogany, with an old wall paper which had fascinated Dolores from her childhood. Leaning willows and little marble bridges, and ladies and gentlemen wandering in groves, their once bright colors faded, their romance unfinished. Against one wall there were white bookcases filled with saccharine romances and gentle essays—relics of her cousins' girlhood. Behind these books in their dim bindings others were hidden; new books, very daring philosophy, poetry, fiction . . . Peter's books, without which she could not have endured the winter just passed.

She took up her pen and poised it over the page. But she did not write. She was thinking . . . he'll come soon. She was thinking . . . in a week, perhaps, I'll see him! She was remembering the way his hair grew, brown hair with a rusty glint of red. She was remembering his eager eyes, gray as steel, set under brows, tilted like wings. She was remembering his height, the breadth of his shoulders, and the way he moved his hands when he grew excited, talking of all he would accomplish, of the world he would conquer.

A flush rose to stain her smooth pallor. In her slim throat a pulse beat, faintly. The last time she had seen Peter—when he came to say good-by, after Christmas—he had kissed her. They'd stood a minute on the railed "deck" on the roof and looked out over stark trees black against a starry sky. From that lookout men had watched the ships come in, laden with fragrant cargo. And as they had stood there, he'd taken her in his arms and bending his head had kissed the warm hollow at her throat. And then, a little awkwardly, but very sweetly, he had kissed her mouth. And in silence they had left the deck and gone

12

downstairs, leaving behind them the dark night, and the still trees, and the smell of snow, and the thrilled light of stars.

He'd not mentioned it in his letters. Yet his letters had changed—almost imperceptibly.

She rose, pushing the paper and pen aside. She couldn't write him. She'd wait until he came. The room darkening with coming night, and heavier fog, she turned on a reading light, and going to her shelves pulled out half a dozen volumes, scattered them to the polished floor, thrust her hand, and drew out a book.

Replacing the innocuous literature of another day she sat down in a wing chair and opened the book. But her mind was not upon Ellen Key. In a week she would see Peter. . . .

Downstairs the two elderly women sat drowsing before their early supper. Letty tiptoed in to turn on the shaded lamps. Miss Carolyn, nodding above her embroidery, hardly heard her enter, while Sarah—motionless—sat lost in her twilight dreams.

Overhead, Ellen Key lay neglected on the floor. Dolores, her young limbs relaxed, her eyes closed, lay back against the cushions of her chair and dreamed too of life, of sunlight too bright for endurance, of freedom, unbearably desired . . . and of Peter.

CHAPTER II

DOLORES was in the garden kneeling by the spring borders. Over her straight linen dress a shapeless sweater was belted. Her head was bare and a streak of brown soil decorated one cheek. She was clipping away the stalks that had already faded. In a flat basket on the ground beside her lay the newly flowered blossoms she had selected for the house. A stretch of lawn beside her was vivid with blossoms growing in an untrammeled freedom. She laid the shears aside, and bending over a great clump of daffodils breathed deeply of the fragrance that rose from them like incense.

In the blue April sky there were little wind-driven white clouds. The sunlight poured down, benevolent and sustaining. She felt the blood run warm in her very fingertips.

A car drove down the quiet street. Dimly, through the mindless moment, as she knelt there absorbing young April into her soul and body, she heard the sound of the engine, of carelessly applied brakes . . . and then, footsteps, running.

She turned. Peter Comstock was coming through the wicket gate into the garden enclosure. For an instant she sat back on her heels and looked at him without a word of greeting. She could not believe him real—yet he seemed a part of the April morning.

Then as he called to her she sprang up and ran to him. "Peter! Peter!"

He took both her grimy hands in his own, laughed, and

14

producing a large white handkerchief, wiped the earthy streak from her face.

"Don't you ever wash, Dolores?"

"No . . . But why are you here? So soon . . . it isn't time, is it? . . . and why didn't you telephone? . . . Oh, Peter, I'm so glad to see you!"

"Not any gladder than I am to be here. . . . Are the Dragons at home?"

"Peter—such friendly dragons—No, Cousin Carolyn is marketing, and Cousin Sarah is closeted with the charity committee at the parish house."

"Let's go in then," he suggested, looking down at her from his great height. "I have something to tell you."

His voice deepened, roughened. Walking beside him to the house she experienced a moment of apprehension. His face looked thinner, fine drawn, older. The gray eyes were blank steel—there was no light in them—she missed the dancing mischief she had known for more than ten years.

"Has anything happened?"

"Plenty," he said briefly, and swung along beside her, his hat in his hand, the sunshine glinting from the close, controlled waves of rusty brown hair.

She took him through the French windows into the drawing room, and from there to a sun porch used as a breakfast room. This was now almost the only entirely modern room in the house. It was furnished in wicker and chintz, the sun poured through the enclosing glass, and it was bright with flowering plants.

"Wait here—a minute—while I put my flowers in water?"

When she had left him he lighted a cigarette and lay back in a long chair, frowning. All the way over— racing in the little car—he had rehearsed what he would say. How would she take it? Would she be disappointed? Would she be understanding? But then—he thought gratefully—she had always understood.

When she came back her hair was ordered, the sweater had disappeared. He looked at her and the gray eyes kindled. She was lovelier every time he saw her. He'd never given another girl a thought.

She sat down near, and leaned forward, her hands clasped between her round knees, her eyes intent.

"What is it, Peter?"

"I'm not going back to college," he answered abruptly, his rehearsals forgotten.

"Peter!"

Her look questioned, and a slow flush burned up in her cheeks. She asked slowly:

"You've not been? . . ."

"Kicked out?" He interrupted. "Not exactly. My father has taken me out for good."

"But, why, Peter? *Why?*"

Her mouth drooped like that of a hurt, bewildered child. Peter was happy in college, she knew.

"It's this way," he answered, a little awkwardly, "I—I've been gambling. Oh, not much. Father found out. Remember David Hatch? Just around the corner from us at home? He's in my class, and was with me on several parties. He lost quite a lot. His allowance didn't cover it, so he had to write home. Old Hatch spoke to my father about it. That was all. I had a letter . . . come home at once. So I came. He was pretty wild. I didn't have to ask him for money. I hadn't lost anything to speak of, and I have my small income from mother. But if I'd won a fortune it would have amounted to the same thing. You know how he feels about cards, and drinking, and even dancing. He's about a hundred years behind the times. Anyway, he said it was evident I was being ruined by loose companions, and too much liberty, and I would kindly arrange to have my things sent after me and stay at home from now on and go into the mills. Overalls and a tin pail."

Dolores said, after a minute:

"You'll hate that, Peter . . ."

He tossed his cigarette to the tiled floor and set his heel on it.

"Yes—what else can I do?"

She did not answer. Young Comstock said, briefly:

"Everybody will know, of course. Taken out of college! Punished, like a kid. Nice for me, isn't it? Not that I care

16

so much about that, but I've always hated the mills, Dolores, greedy, cruel things. . . . To have to drudge there, day in, day out . . . like being caught in a trap. There's no use telling father . . . he wouldn't understand. The mills mean everything to him. More than I do," he added youthfully, bitterly.

"Oh, no, Peter he *does* care for you. You're all he has," Dolores contradicted him, without much conviction.

"You don't really believe that! You're just saying it. In the first place . . ." He broke off and jumped to his feet, crying, "He's old, Dolores, old . . . and I'm young! Sixty and nineteen! He might be my grandfather! He knows it. He resents it. He hasn't forgiven my mother for dying because she couldn't endure that gloomy house and his elderly friends. Why she married him God only knows. A childless widower, so much older than herself . . . it was incredible. It wasn't fair to her . . . or to me."

He fell silent, thinking of his mother who had died when he was small. She had been blonde and slender, and had moved through the dark, high-ceilinged rooms like a spear of sunlight. Peter had not been too young to watch her fade, repressed and dominated, until she was a little lonely shadow. Ashabel Comstock had treated her as if she were a thoughtless child. He had not even allowed her to change the house—to impress her own personality upon it. She had slept at his side in the great sleigh bed in which her predecessor had lain. The massive furniture, the linen, the china, and the silver had all been the marriage portion of the first Mrs. Comstock. Inanimate and malicious, their weight had crushed the second wife.

"Have you told him what you wanted to do when you graduated?"

"Yes. I was a fool. 'Write?' he asked. 'You?' And then he laughed. I . . . I saw red for a minute. It was like ice breaking up, that laugh, cold and sliding, and sharp edged. He said 'I'll not have any half-baked, long-haired, ink-stained imbecile for my son. You'll go into the mills.' "

"Peter!"

He dropped down beside her again. Half unconsciously

17

he reached out and took her hand and held it between his own.

"So here I am."

She said, dimly:

"You'll never be able to stand it."

He did not answer her for a second. Then he said, irrelevantly:

"I miss it all so much already."

He was silent, remembering the good times, not removed from him more than two days. . . . Smoke and talk, and eager voices, arguments, noise and laughter, all the great questions of the world and of life settled around a table. Fat old Hodge Meadows sprawling on a rickety divan. Jimmy Morse reading his atrocious poems. Chink Garrod reciting Dobson, Meredith, or making plaintive music on his steel guitar. . . .

Dolores said, hopefully:

"But you'll go on writing. He can't stop you, Peter. He mustn't."

The gray eyes burned.

"No! Dolores, I've an idea for a play. Such an idea! A knockout! I've two notebooks full. I'll bring them over next time I come, and read what I have. You'll like it."

"What's it called?" she asked, glowing with pride in him.

" 'The Trap.' "

" 'The Trap'? Tell me a little."

But he was suddenly boyish, and embarrassed.

"Oh, it wouldn't sound like much, telling. It's about a couple who marry young—you know . . . propinquity, all that sort of thing; and what marriage does to them. The loss of personality, of freedom. The drab days, and the pressure of circumstance. You know—we've talked about it before."

She nodded, gravely. She and Peter had decided, as long ago as last year, that marriage was a failure. They had said that they would never marry—not while the institution remained as it now was.

"You'll write it," she decided, "and it will be a success. Nothing can stop you, really, Peter—neither your father

18

nor the mills. You are *yourself*—you know. You belong to yourself!"

It was their slogan. He looked at her, drew her a little closer by the hand he held. Suddenly they became aware of pulses beating at the contact—of hearts that leaped abruptly and pained them sweetly.

"You always understood," he told her huskily.

When he had gone, leaving her, as he said, to break the news to "the dragons" she went up to her room and sat down on her bed. Her heart was hot with championship for him. Her soul, in silver armor, crusaded under his banner. That wicked old man, his father! It wasn't fair! Why, she thought rebelliously, do old people have such domination over the young? Old people had lived their lives, they must step back for the new generation. But they wouldn't. They meddled, and muddled, and interfered; lectured, and warned and advised. They were like Court of Inquiry—sitting on the case of youth, drowsily, enviously, weighing the evidence—bringing in the verdict of guilty.

You've only one life to live, she thought. Why has anyone any right to tell you how you'll live it? Her eyes filled at the thought of Peter in the mills he hated. Peter with all his laughter and eagerness, and hunger for life and adventure, buried in that dark house with no companion save the austere old man, hard, loveless, humorless as granite. Peter with his talent, his vision, his quick, hot heart.

She twisted her hands. If only she could help him. She burned to stand beside him—shoulder to shoulder—to win through with him to freedom.

He had promised her that he would come over every opportunity he had. The distance was not great. He could come evenings, after his work, and on Saturdays, and perhaps some Sundays. She would see him often.

Perhaps, if he found it difficult to work in the musty, chilly atmosphere of his father's house, he would bring his notebooks over to her. They would go down to the beach and sit in the sunlight against the rotting driftwood, and watch the blue water. She would be so quiet, sitting beside him. He could lie there in the warm sand, weaving his

19

fancies and his plots. They would discuss everything.

Oh, if it weren't for Peter she would die in this quiet house where nothing ever hapened! She would grow old without having lived!

She jumped up and began pulling books out of the shelves. There was something she had meant to ask Peter, a passage she had marked. Carolyn Brewster coming upstairs to call her to luncheon found her on her knees, flushed and dusty, the books heaped around her, some of them open, face up, face down. She exclaimed, from the threshold:

"Dolores! How untidy! Pick the books up, my dear, at once. Wash your face and hands and come downstairs to luncheon."

Her tone was gentle and disapproving. She answered meekly, "Yes, Cousin Carolyn," and started to replace the volumes, shaken with fear lest the older woman come nearer and read some of the titles. If Cousin Carolyn ever knew what she, Dolores, had read in the past year or more! She almost laughed aloud at the thought.

But Carolyn had left the room with her unhurried step.

Dolores rose to her feet. She looked down at the shelves upon which the faded, futile romances guarded the dangerous presence of books which panted and throbbed with life. Romance masking reality, she thought, and the phrase seemed to her dimly symbolic.

Fairy tales were well enough for children. But she was no longer a child. Books . . . and Peter . . . and her own growing maturity had unveiled the world before her unfrightened eyes. She felt a moment's pity for her cousins. They had never looked life in the face. They were content to evade it. They were, she thought, defiantly, a century younger than herself.

She had compassion on their ignorance and their innocence. Running down the stairs, she burst into the dining room like a whirlwind. Cousin Sarah said, indulgently, "Gently, my dear, gently," and Cousin Carolyn drew her slender brows together. What a child she was, the older women thought, looking at her affectionately—what an unthinking child.

20

CHAPTER III

"MAGRUDER reports you incompetent," Ashabel Comstock told his son one May morning.

He leaned back, placed the tips of his thin fingers together, and regarded Peter under shaggy gray brows. His long-chinned face was a mask. Peter looked at him in despair.

"I do my best, sir."

"Possibly. Nevertheless—incompetent, Magruder says. He tells me you take no interest."

Peter was silent. His father continued.

"This business will be yours one day. I have given my life to it, as my father did. I thought that my only son would follow my example."

He paused; and then went on, evenly:

"I am ageing. But I cannot die in peace and know that I am handing over my life work to a gambler, a ne'er-do-well."

Peter's hand flashed out in a gesture of contradiction. His father continued, unheeding:

"You come of God-fearing, sober-living, hard-working stock. If you disgrace your name you'll be the first. You went to college against my will. You were to be a business man, not a professor. I have no use for the universities of to-day. They are hotbeds of laxity, of rebellion, of atheism. But your heart was set on wasting four good years. In my weakness I allowed you your way. You see what has come of it. You have proven that it was not education you desired, but loose living. Have you anything to say for yourself?"

Peter's face had flushed. He stood before the flat topped desk of hideous golden oak, and looked about the bare walls of the small office. The room was drab—strictly utilitarian. He replied slowly:

"I—I've tried to do my best, sir, as I told you. But my heart's not in it. It isn't my job."

"And what is, then?" asked his father, his thin lips contorted in an unpleasant smile.

Peter turned sullen.

"I've told you. I want to go to New York—get a place on a newspaper—I want to learn to write."

Mr. Comstock balanced a paper knife between his fingers.

"You think you have talent?"

"I do!" said Peter defiantly.

"In the old days," his father mused, "writing was an honorable profession. But the Emersons and Longfellows are dead. The world is full of young fools who scribble dangerous trash. I've seen some of the books you read, Peter. Perfumed dynamite, flouting standards, mocking decency. You'll never set pen to paper with my consent. Do you think I'd have my name dragged through the slime and mire of the public prints of to-day? You'll go on with your work at the mills. You'll try and make a man of yourself. Magruder will give you another chance. That's all I have to say."

He turned to his letters and pressed a button to call the elderly, worried-looking man, who served as stenographer-secretary. The mills were run along old-fashioned lines. They were good mills and they made money, but they made very little effort to compete with modern methods of advertising and efficiency.

Peter left the room and returned to work. His heart was as sore with shame and anger as if it had been physically bruised.

When he reached home that evening he went to his room without seeing his father. He hated the room. It was papered in a sickening chocolate-brown, the furniture had sudden corners against which a lonely boy had often scraped his little shins. In the corner stood a child's school-desk. Peter went to it and pulled out the drawers where his notes were kept. They were empty.

He searched the room—anxious and unsuspecting. What on earth had he done with them?

They were nowhere to be found. He washed, changed, and went down to supper. The meal was served and eaten in silence. Mr. Comstock read the local paper and never opened his mouth except to pronounce a blessing at the beginning and end of the meal.

When it was over he rose and said, quietly:

"I'll see you in my library."

Peter's heart sank. He wanted to get out the car and drive over to see Dolores that evening. But he followed his father into the dark, leather-smelling room without a word. Hadn't he said enough? Damn that old finicking Magruder anyway!

On the way he saw a letter on the hall table which he had overlooked on his return from work. He knew the writer of that sprawling hand. Hodge Meadows. A wave of nostalgia swept over him for the rooms at college. the talk of young men, the laughter and the tolerance. He put the letter in his pocket and went into the library.

His father was standing by the beautiful mantel, the only gracious thing in the room. A fire burned for the night had turned cool. The hearth was full of charred paper, now and then a little white ash drifted out over the screen, eddied aimlessly and settled on floor or table.

"Sit down."

Peter obeyed. He drew out a cigarette case, lighted a cigarette. His father frowned, heavily.

"I do not approve of smoking. However . . ." He stopped, cleared his throat and went on:

"When I returned home to-night I went to your room. I opened your desk. I removed from the drawer your note-books and your pages of manuscript. You write an atrocious hand. But I was determined to give you your chance. You tell me that it is your ambition to write. Very well. You have never honored me with your confidence. I did not know on what lines your vaunted talent manifested itself. I brought your scribblings here and read them through. If I could discern a single spark—I told myself—I would compromise with you in some way and give you your opportunity." He motioned toward the fireplace, and his controlled voice rose slightly. "There lies your blasphemy, in ashes."

Peter, white with rage, sprang to his feet.

"You . . . you *burned* . . . ? You had no right!"

"I am your father. You are not of age."

"I don't care if you're my father twenty times over," Peter shouted. "It's not my fault that you are! And it gives you no right to pry into my affairs and destroy my personal property!"

"Moderate your tone," commanded his father, sternly. "I will not have such stuff under my roof. You jeer at every institution sacred to God and man. You have no morals. This book that I found filled with notes for a play—'The Trap,' I think it was called. A hysterical defiance of marriage . . . an open advocating of lawless union. . . . There it is, in the fireplace. You'll not write another line in my house. You'll keep your filthy thoughts to yourself and not soil good paper with them. The seeds of corruption are in you. But I'll not let you go to your destruction without making a fight for your immortal soul. Kneel down!" he thundered, suddenly.

Peter shaking, ashen, looked up as his father towered over him. Both were very tall, but the elder man was the taller. He raised a clinched fist and menaced his son, his somber eyes, gray as Peter's, burning with a fanatic light under the drawn brows. So had Ashabel's ancestors looked when they sent the soft, young witches to the stake . . .

"Kneel down, I say!"

Mechanically Peter knelt. He was almost unconscious of so doing. He was shaken to his very core. He was bewildered, blind with rage, and with authentic sorrow. His work destroyed, gone for nothing! The work that had meant so much to him, into which he had put his dreams and his visions and his rebellions.

His father knelt stiffly, by the desk. Peter heard his high

24

monotonous voice raised in belligerent supplication. The words escaped him, for the blood drumming his ears. Occasionally he heard a phrase dimly.

"Set his footsteps on the path of rectitude, O Lord! Save him from his sinful thoughts, his unclean heart. Have mercy on this, my only son."

Silence fell, hard and abrupt as a blow.

"Get up," said Comstock, on his feet. "Go to your room. We'll say no more of this. You know my wishes. God help you!"

Peter left the room without looking toward his father. His mouth worked and he staggered slightly. He had passed through the most dreadful moment of his life, and he was sick with his own emotion.

When he had gone Comstock sat down heavily at his desk. He was trembling. He pulled open a drawer, thrust in his shaking hand, took out a photograph, laid it before him and looked at it.

It was the picture of a young girl, slender, and blonde. She had laughter in her eyes and at the corners of her mouth. Her face looked back at the old man, trusting, happy. It had been taken before her marriage to him.

"Ellie," he muttered strangely, "I want to do what's right for the boy. Your boy."

The granite face broke up into lines of tenderness. He touched the picture gently with a hard forefinger. He had never understood her. He had broken her upon the wheel of his austere, repressed passion. He had loved her terribly. He loved her son.

Much later he went heavily up the stairs and tried the door of Peter's room. It was locked. He listened at the threshold. There was no sound. He turned and went to his own room—his shoulders stooped—his feet dragging.

Peter's room was empty. He had reached it, somehow, flung himself on the bed. He had sobbed there, once or twice, dryly, hurtingly. Then he rose, locked the door, took a cap from a wardrobe and opened his window. It was an easy climb down to the roof of the porch, and from there down the pillar to the ground. Reaching the scented darkness he made a circuitous tour of the house and gained the barn, some distance from the house. There his car waited, static.

Presently he drove down the back road, through a lane bordered with apple trees to the main road. He stepped on the accelerator and sped off, the wind in his hot face.

It was fairly late when he reached the house on Pleasant Street. He parked the car and ran up the steps. The door opened, seemingly of itself.

"I heard you come," Dolores told him breathlessly. "Peter, what is the matter?"

He asked her, hoarsely:

"Where are your people?"

"Cousin Carolyn is in bed with a sick-headache," she answered, wondering, apprehensive, "and Cousin Sarah is out . . . Peter, what is it?"

"Come out here," he begged her, "I . . . I . . . can't bear to be in a house. . . ."

She followed, wordless. They went silently into the garden and beyond to the peach orchard where a double swing stood; a battered thing, the green paint worn.

In this swing Dolores and Peter had travelled thousands of miles in their childhood. They had swung through blossom time, through fruit time, through autumn leaves; to China, to India, to fairyland. . . .

Now they sat down, side by side, and the old swing creaked under their weight. It rocked them gently as a cradle. All about them was the smell of green leaves budding, of damp, fecund earth, of wind and starlight. Fragrance rose from shubbery and bulb borders, from grass and earth. The tinted petals of peach blow drifted idly past.

"Peter?"

He reached out and took her hand, clung to it.

"I'm through," he said.

"What do you mean?" she asked evenly, but her heart was cold with terror.

"I'm going to get out . . . away . . . anywhere . . . where he'll never find me. . . ."

"Your . . . father?"

"Don't call him that!"

26

"Peter, what has he done?"

"He burned them," answered Peter, as if in wonder. "Everything; the verse, the sketches, the notes for the play. Everything. Ashes, there in the library hearth. . . . He . . . Oh, I can't tell you what he said and did. I'm not to write another line, he said. . . ."

Peter laughed, angrily.

"He might as well tell me not to breathe!"

"Peter, what shall you do?"

"Go away, I tell you. . . . I'll get a job somehow. I've some money and I can sell the car. It's mine. I bought it myself. It won't bring much—it wasn't new when I got it—" he planned, "but it will help. If he thinks that I'll stay any longer than I have to to pack and get off . . . He reminded me that I wasn't of age. As if I needed reminding! But I'll go where he can never find me. . . . New York's a big city."

After a moment she said in a low voice:

"You'll be leaving me, Peter. . . ."

She felt him turn in the starry darkness. She heard him say:

"I know. I hadn't thought . . ."

"But you must think," she said suddenly. "You're all I have."

Then his arms went out and took her within their strong young circle. He drew her dark head against his breast and leaned his mouth to hers. At the kiss which held so much of parting and despair the divine earth flame leaped up between them, welded them together. They clung there, mouth to mouth, heart to heart, while the peach blossoms drifted about their young, thrilled bodies.

"You can't leave me, Peter," she said, sobbing, "I couldn't endure it without you. Peter, take me with you. . . ."

CHAPTER IV

AFTER a long time he said, holding her close:

"Take you with me? Do you know what that will mean?"

She turned her cheek to his shoulder, loving the scent and feel of the rough tweed coat:

"Yes. . . . Freedom. We love each other, we'll be free together."

At the word, the brave word, in her lovely voice, his heart leaped like a wild thing.

"Free . . ." he repeated slowly.

"You'll work," she told him softly, "and I'll work too. I'll help you. I'll learn to type all your manuscripts. We'll find some place to live. We will choose our own friends, people who understand. I'll leave you unhampered, Peter. You needn't feel the least obligation toward me. You'll just love me . . . and be free. We'll never be like the other people, married people who grow tired and restless, and hate each other. We'll be ourselves. Workers. Lovers. You and I. It will be wonderful. . . ."

He asked her, his voice breaking:

"You've the courage? You won't be *sorry?*"

"Sorry? With you? Courage? But I love you, Peter. Tell me you love me . . . you've not said it, yet."

He said it over and over, his young mouth on her young mouth. The stars looked down upon them, ironic and indifferent. Only the little May wind understood and pitied, blowing by, with peach bloom on its wings.

"Your play, Peter, your great play. Never mind the notes. It will all come back, and more. And, we'll have the bravery to live your belief. Real marriage is comradeship, work, liberty . . . letting each other alone . . . loving . . . not clinging."

After a long time he said:

"Ah, bless you, Dolores . . . with you to help me and to love me, I'll justify everything."

Sitting there, they made their plans. Peter would go home, pack what he needed, take the car to another town and sell it. Dolores would leave her cousins' ostensibly on a visit to Boston. It could be easily managed. They would meet at any appointed place, and go to New York.

"Your cousins?" he asked once.

She laughed. She was young; she was in love; she was escaping from her cage.

"They'll be sorry. They'll never understand. But it doesn't matter. Why should we sacrifice ourselves for old people who have already lived? They've been good to me, Peter, but they've never loved me much. They took me, as a duty. Well, now they're free of me. I've a little money untouched in the savings bank. There will be more, when I'm eighteen."

He said:

"We'll manage."

"I won't be a drag on you, Peter!"

"Drag? You will be my inspiration! You always have been. There's never been any one else. Only you."

Later, their pitiful plans completed, she went to the car with him. Putting his hand in his pocket for the key he found the unopened letter from Meadows. He drew it out, standing under a street light, and broke the seal. He looked down the scrawled sheet and his face lighted with excitement. There was an enclosure. He weighed this in his hand.

"It's from Meadows, my room-mate at college. He's sending me a note to his uncle—city editor on the *Star*—in case I ever need it, he says. Before I left college we talked about my getting a job there sometime. And I've written him since . . . said I didn't think I could stick it here long."

"I knew you'd have your chance," she told him confidently.

Five minutes later she turned back into the house. She was not the same Dolores who had come to the door at the sound of the car. This was a woman, tremulous and gallant, groping in the darkness for her happiness, dreaming she had found it, that she held it fast.

Lying in bed she told herself that she was hurting no one. She was giving herself to her beloved, a free gift. She would work for and with him. There would never be a truer marriage. Could laws and churches marry them more than they were already married in their hearts? She turned on the pillows and rested her hot cheek against the cool linen. To be with Peter, on any terms; to leave him unfettered; to be his star, shining always, never dimming, through custom and habit. She asked for nothing else, remembering the dark and hushed orchards, the feel of his coat against her face, the touch of his hands, the flaming of his lips, the fragrance of spring.

His ancestors and hers had been pioneers. They would be pioneers, too, in the new world waiting for them.

Peter drove home, his heart singing. A job in prospect, Dolores, a leaving of everything he hated and feared. Life was excellent, was wonderful and he would be a part of its great, restless heart; never to stagnate, or to watch himself grow old, his dreams fading, his hopes perishing. Just to live every moment, to do good work, to love and be loved, fearless and free.

Reaching the barn he put up the car and went to his room by the way he had left it. It was as he left it, cool and dark, the door locked. He grinned like a small boy, and getting out of his clothes crawled into bed and lay there, his arms behind his head.

Not many more nights now, here in this drab room. Not many more nights . . .

He flushed, cleanly, turned and closed his eyes. Oh, Dolores, oh, freedom, oh, beauty of youth and spring!

"I need some shoes and things," Dolores announced at

30

breakfast, "and I wonder if it would be all right if I went to Boston? Anna Adams has asked me."

That was quite true. Anna, a little older than Dolores, and an old associate, had given a standing invitation.

Cousin Sarah and Cousin Carolyn regarded each other doubtfully. Dolores did not visit much. However, Anna was a nice child and a proper companion, and Anna's mother a relative. Why not, if the child was as set upon going as she seemed to be? She looked from one to the other, her eyes darkly pleading.

"We'll see," promised Carolyn, wan from her headache.

Later, they consulted. It might be well if Dolores went away for a time. Peter was coming over too often. Of course, if it came to anything, the cousins would be pleased. But it was too soon yet. Peter had his way to make, now that his father was ailing and needed him, and had taken him out of the University for that reason . . . which was the cousins' version of Peter's sudden reappearance.

Yes, Delores might go to Boston.

There was a slight hitch in Dolores' plans. For Cousin Carolyn wired her relative and the relative wired back . . . delighted . . . what day and train . . . ?

Dolores conferred with Peter. He came over a day or so later, on a Saturday. He hadn't much to tell. He'd written Meadows he would be down shortly to present the letter to Meadows' uncle. He had arranged for the sale of the car. What was this about Boston?

"I'l have to go, Peter. I need only stay a few days. I'd be on my way back, you see. It would be perfectly simple. I can write after we get to New York. I'll leave the day of my return vague."

"All right."

"Your father?"

"He hasn't spoken to me, except formally. I've hardly seen him."

Early the following week Dolores went to Boston. Her cousins took her to the station. Neither saw her turn at the gate while the taxi waited to look back at the house.

31

Her little handbag contained all she could take from her room. She had packed her books, and expressed them to herself in Boston. She had gone to the bank and drawn out the money.

Now she looked back. For the last time. She could see through the gate into the garden enclosure. She could see the curtains swaying at the windows of her bedroom. She raised her eyes to the roof deck from which her people had watched their ships come in. Good-by, she said in her heart, and felt how rough her throat grew, how it ached . . . *Good-by.* . . .

At the station she clung momently to the two women, kissing them again and again.

"Good-by . . . you've been so good . . ." she murmured, incoherently.

When the train had pulled out and they could no longer see her waving from the window they still stood there and looked at each other and away again, touched, unaccountably disturbed.

"It's lonely here for her, I suppose," Sarah said, walking back to the taxi. "She's glad to get away for a little."

"She's very emotional," Carolyn commented, slowing her long steps to her sister's pace, "I'm sure she doesn't get it from the Brewsters."

They thought of that Spanish girl whose portrait hung in the gilt and blue drawing-room and they sighed. Blood like that complicated things, made life uncomfortable for its possessor and for those about her. Dolores was very young. She would marry and settle down.

Anna met Dolores at the train and flung her arms about her.

"I'm so glad you came," said Anna, a blonde, plump eighteen, sentimental and volatile. "We'll do a matinée and shop. There's a dance, too."

"I haven't an evening gown," Dolores began, and remembered the thick roll of bills that she had hidden away, "but I'll buy one."

Anna's house on Beacon Street was charming. Anna's mother was gentle and fussy, her father abstracted and good-natured. Boston was looking its best in the springtime. The Common was bright with flowers, the swan boats glided over the lake. Dolores lived dreaming through the days. Would the time never come when she could go *home . . . ?*

She bought more clothes than she had ever purchased at one time. Anna teased her:

"As if you were planning a trousseau," she said.

"I shall never marry," replied Dolores serenely, and went on buying. Anna laughed at her again, blue eyed, dimpled.

"What nonsense! With your looks! I told you what Fred Sears said at the dance."

"Tell me again!" urged Dolores, light hearted.

"Prettiest girl he'd ever seen. He's making a tour of the Cape next summer . . . he's going to stop off to see you on his way."

"How nice!" said Dolores, and her heart sang . . . he'll never find me, no one will ever find me again . . . we're going to live on a desert island . . . Peter and I . . .

She hadn't a misgiving. She had set her hand to the plough, she would not turn back, even to look over her slim shoulder at all she was leaving, relinquishing, forever.

When she left Anna took her to the station. Dolores had had to buy new luggage for her purchases and her books. Anna had been curious about the books.

"What are they?"

"Just books. I suppose the express office forwarded them by mistake."

Anna nodded, satisfied. She had not looked at the tag in Dolores' handwriting.

At the first station Dolores left the train and took the next one back to Boston. There, in the station Peter waited. He came toward her, both hands out, his eyes shining.

"It's been years."

Oh, if she'd had a misgiving, little or big, would it not have vanished at the sight and touch of him?

The first train they could get to New York would bring them in at night. They had their dinner aboard, watching the country slide by, looking at each other over the little table, as the car swayed and the chinaware rattled, and the water in the glasses was agitated into miniature waves.

"Meadows is in town. He's been fired or something," said said Peter with a grin. "He was always pretty wild. Perhaps he'll go to the *Star* office with me."

"Peter, I've bought such a lot of things!"

"You have . . . what, for instance, darling?"

At the little word, the dear word, her heart hurt her. She looked at him in silence. Peter caught his breath and felt himself drowning in the dark warm pool of her eyes.

"Oh, just things. An evening dress, a daytime dress . . . and . . ."

"I want to buy your dresses!" said Peter jealously.

"No . . . maybe special times as surprises. But that isn't our bargain. I must . . . must keep myself. I'm going to find a job too, you know. There must be something I can do."

He was silent. Somehow he didn't like it. Women in his family had never "found jobs." It was not in his blood to approve of the innovation. But she was right . . . they had made their compact—each was to be free.

They reached New York rather late and stood in the roar and bustle of the station, two bewildered children, their hands seeking each other's for reassurance and comfort.

CHAPTER V

DOLORES murmured, involuntarily:

"Peter! I'm afraid . . ."

He did not hear her. People milled about them, intent upon their own concerns. Their porters shuffled impatiently, asking, at intervals, "Taxi? Where to sir?"

"Taxi, of course," said Peter irritably, and followed the stoop shouldered men, with Dolores almost running to keep up with him. He was inwardly confused. It had seemed so simple, so inevitable. Now that it had, so to speak, happened, these details cropped up, blunting the fine edge of his resolution. Stations and porters, taxis and hotels—somehow he had omitted to include these minor annoyances in his calculations.

He gave the driver the name of the first hotel which came to him, the hotel at which he had stopped when he came down from college with his friends. At least, he reflected, they would know him there.

He turned to Dolores. Her oval face was a pallid blur in the temporary darkness. As they shot into brilliant light and he saw how dilated her eyes were, heard her quick breathing, he took her hand in his own and held it, finding it very cold.

"We'll have to say you're my sister," he began nervously.

"Oh, Peter, no . . . no . . ." she wailed, astonishingly.

"But why? What else can we do?"

"I don't know. It seems all wrong somehow. Starting out that way. I hate it."

"So do I," he muttered uncomfortably, "but we can't do anything else. . . ."

She said nothing. Her throat was full of tears. She took her hand from his and twisted it in the other. It was all so strange. So . . . unromantic. So utterly without the high drumbeat of adventure.

They reached the hotel and went in, preceded by agile youths who seized their bags. At the desk a clerk who remembered Peter was free to attend to them. He was a clever clerk, and made it his business to remember people . . . particularly young men with mill owning fathers.

Peter was no actor. He stammered something about . . . "my sister."

The clerk said, smoothly:

"I am so very sorry, Mr. Comstock. We all all filled up. There are two conventions in town, you know."

Sister! It had not needed more than a flicker of a sandy Scotch eyelash toward Dolores to give the cue to the clerk. She was pale, terribly excited, holding herself in leash by an effort. And Peter's face was set, obstinacy overlying embarrassment. Of course, it might be perfectly all right. An eloping couple? But there was no ring upon Dolores' ungloved hand. Mr. Comstock, the elder, was a powerful man. And the clerk was fond of his job. Therefore he murmured, shrugging slightly . . . "sorry."

Peter said something, anything, turned and marched out with Dolores at his heels, and the porters following with the bags.

They took another taxi. Peter, on the curb, said desperately to the driver:

"Could you find us a quiet hotel?"

The driver, also astute in his way, nodded briefly. He had, he thought, sized up his pair. Gentlefolk. The bags were placed in the car, the impassive porters feed, the cab drove off.

"Well!" began Peter in a fury.

Dolores was whimpering softly, like a bruised child.

"He looked . . . did you see how he *looked?*" she asked, stifled.

Peter said nothing. He put his arms about her shoulder

36

and drew her close for comfort, his own and hers. She leaned against him, and nuzzled her cheek against his shoulder. There was no passion in the way they clung, each to the other, there was hardly tenderness. It was the groping of childish hands to ward off fear of the dark.

They reached the hotel, near Central Park. It was small and old and shabby, and very respectable. A clerk thrust the register toward them, Peter signed awkwardly, and they went up in a creaking elevator and were ushered into two great echoing rooms, a bath between. Their escort departed, leaving them alone.

Peter stood at Dolores' doorway and said, self-consciously:

"Don't unpack or anything. To-morrow we'll find some place to live. You must be awfully tired."

She said, kneeling on the floor beside a handbag:

"I keep thinking . . . Cousin Carolyn and Cousin Sarah . . . they'll begin to worry."

"We'll write . . . to-morrow . . ." He shifted from one foot to another and said again, "You must be tired . . . Good night. . . ."

She rose and stood there, her hands at her sides, and looked at him appealingly. He came in, took her in his arms and kissed her. And she said again, as she had said at the station, "Peter, I'm afraid. . . ."

He answered, huskily:

"Darling, you needn't be."

A moment later he went back into his own room. Doors were shut between them. Dolores undressed, shivering in the warm May wind that blew through a window. She crept into the creaking single bed and lay there, shaking as if she had a chill.

Street lights made pools on the floor. The room was loud with echoes, street noises, her own heart beating. She clenched her hands under the covers. What was she doing here? Why had she come? She thought of the look in the eye of that other hotel clerk, of his butter-sauve voice. Suddenly she was sick for her own place and her own people. Her own room with the smell of salt and flowers invading her dreams, her low slipper chair, her books, her bed, the trees outside her window, safety, bondage, peace. . . .

Not far away from her Peter lay awake. He was sick with self-disgust. The hot blood of adventure had cooled. This was sheer madness, he thought, tossing on his pillows.

Finally they slept, lost children, lonely and unhappy.

The morning was May itself. Peter, rising early, bathed and shaved and dressed. With sunlight, his mood had changed. It would be all right. It had to be. They had brought such high hopes, such resolves to this adventure. He wondered if Dolores slept. He hoped so, and went about his preparations softly, lest he wake her. He thought of her lying there, her face faintly flushed with sleep, her dark eyes closed, the lashes making little shadows on her cheeks, her scarlet mouth carven to a dim dreaming smile. His heart threatened to choke him. She was his, entrusted to him, his comrade in the new freedom.

When he was ready he knocked softly at her door:
"Dolores?"

There was no answer. He knocked again, louder.
"Dolores?"

He listened. Not a sound or stirring. He knew an immediate fear. Had she left him? Where had she gone?

He opened the door. The room was empty.

Peter went downstairs—stopped at the desk. The day clerk regarded him incuriously.

"My sister? A young lady—tall, dark . . . have you seen her go out?"

The clerk reassured him.

Yes. She had given him her room key. She had left the hotel, not many minutes earlier.

Peter went hatless into the streets which were cool and faintly scented with growing things from the nearness of the Park. She hadn't run away. Her bags were still as she'd left them.

Then he saw her, across the street, walking swiftly toward the Park. He ran, reckless of appearance, caught up with her, gasping:

"Dolores! You frightened me to death . . . to find you gone!"

"I couldn't sleep," she said, "I got up very early and

38

dressed. And sat in the room. Then I came out. I had to—I couldn't stay indoors."

"Breakfast," he began, but she silenced him with a little foreign gesture.

"Let's walk, Peter."

They went, in silence and side by side, deep into the greening Park. The shrubs were blossoming, early flowers laughed from the beds, there were lilacs breaking into plumed purple bloom. Finally, a little afraid of their own silence, they sat down on a bench and he heard her sigh.

"Peter?"

"Yes?"

"You know I love you?"

Tenderness flooded him. He reached out, took her hand, felt his pulses throb under her touch. It was May. It was morning. They loved each other. What else mattered?

"I can't go on," she said, very low.

"Dolores!"

She twisted around, faced him, her cheeks flushed, her eyes bright with withheld tears.

"I'm a coward. . . . I can't face it. . . . That other clerk at the hotel . . . and here . . . last night. . . . It was dreadful. I'll have to go home, I'm not brave enough, Peter."

"But you can't go," he said stupidly, "we've burned our bridges behind us. You'll never be able to explain."

"I shall, somehow. It doesn't matter."

The voices of her ancestors cried out within her. She could not go on. Freedom was a word. Even that Spanish girl who had followed her man over unknown seas to an unknown and uncongenial land had held to tradition. The salty blood of God-fearing, sea-faring men ran chillingly in her veins with the tempered blood of noble, clear-eyed women who had nothing to fear and had never known shame.

Peter sighed, deeply. Yet a curious relief crept through him. He asked, low:

"You'd . . . give me up?"

39

Her eyes widened at that. Give him up? Peter? All she had, all she had ever wanted?

"No . . . no. . . ."

Her voice, dark velvet, was broken. They were alone, it seemed, in the dim misty green spaces of the Park. No one passed. He took her in his arms and laid his lips on hers. The lovely flame rushed upward, fused them, held them, shook them terribly. Clasping arms and a long kiss. What else mattered? They couldn't be parted, ever.

He said, brokenly:

"Darling . . . don't cry . . . let's go back to the hotel . . . and . . . then . . . we'll be married."

"Married?"

She wrenched herself away, regarded him strangely, a sob broke from her.

"Married? After all we've said . . . and believed . . .?"

"There's no other way," Peter answered.

After a long moment she turned and put her hand on his.

"I'm sorry," she said, quaintly. "We hadn't meant it so. . . ."

"I can't get along without you," he told her, his young brows drawn.

After a moment she asked, as once he had asked her:

"You won't be afraid . . . or sorry?"

"No."

"Peter, I won't hamper you. Just as if . . . as if we weren't . . . you understand. It will be the same. . . ."

Presently they walked back to their hotel and ate their breakfast in a dim room hung with faded red velvet and decorated with tarnished gilt. Peter said, watching her pour the coffee:

"You have the loveliest hands. . . . We'll be married to-day. . . . I don't know how one goes about it. I'll call up Hodge Meadows. . . . He knows everything."

Later, he was a long time at the telephone. When he came back he was smiling, and embarrassed.

"He's coming up. He says you have to wait in New York. Something about a residence. It's all right," he added

40

quickly, as he saw her face full, "he said something about Port Chester."

"Port Chester?"

"Yes, I don't know anything about it. Hodge will be along soon. We can pack and get ready."

When she was in her own room, changing her frock for one of the new ones, she looked long into the mirror. Her wedding day. She hadn't thought of it like that. She'd imagined . . . but what had she imagined? Or had she imagined nothing, just taken the step ahead, blindly, confident in the courage that had failed her?

Young Meadows, rotund and genial, arrived with a car, another man and two girls. He said, as they all gathered in the lobby:

"I've always wanted to officiate at an elopement. If I had the nerve myself . . . how about it, Coralie?"

Coralie, blonde and giggling, shook her head at him: "Not for me," she said gaily.

He'd brought the others along, he explained, for "a party."

They piled Peter and Dolores into the big open car and tossed their bags in after them. They sat with Meadows in the front seat, the light hearted strangers smoking and laughing behind them.

"Where you going, after?" Meadows inquired, twisting through traffic.

"We hadn't thought. We'll have to get an apartment or something."

"No honeymoon?" asked Peter's friend in amazement. "But that won't do!"

Peter laughed, uncomfortably.

"I have to get a job. I thought . . . your uncle . . ."

"I'll take you to see him. He'll give you something. Why don't you and Dolores . . . you don't mind my calling her that . . . ? stop over at Briarcliff over Sunday? I'll speak to the Old Man meantime."

Peter turned toward the girl. She was sitting erect, her hands in her lap, her eyes unseeing.

"You'd like that?"

She nodded. She had not really heard him.

They came to Port Chester. The formalities took little time. Meadows had warned them both, "You'll have to fix up about your age, you know . . . on the license."

It had been done. Peter Comstock, aged twenty-one. Dolores Brewster, aged eighteen. A magistrate married them.

Late luncheon and their healths drunk in the contents of two flasks. Laughter and joking comments which made Dolores a little unhapy. Then, in the afternoon, the hills of Briarcliff and the great hotel.

The "wedding party" left them, calling out blessings. Peter and Dolores walked into the lobby. He signed the register, with a firm hand:

"Mr. and Mrs. Peter Comstock."

While the clerk turned to get the key they looked at each other. It was done. They were married. They had not meant to be. Life had forced them into this situation, life and the warning voices of past generations.

Peter smiled at his wife.

"Shall we go upstairs?"

After all, they had each other.

CHAPTER VI

MAY sponsored their mating. The green hills of Briarcliff, where mauve and rosy shadows lay in the hollows, the budding of trees in which the sap ran free, made the setting for their romance. They woke to misty mornings and a far glimpse of silver waters, to birds that choired at their windows, to flushing skies and the marvellous sense of each other's nearness.

They had sent wires from Port Chester, to the old man in the gloomy house who waited, pondering Peter's absence, not believing it other than an escapade undertaken in temper, and to the cousins, who had wakened to a slow worry . . . why hadn't Dolores come home?

Letters reached them before they left Briarcliff where their few days had been sweetly prolonged to a week. Cousin Carolyn wrote reproachfully, without bitterness. She was hurt and disappointed. Why had not Dolores confided in her? Surely she knew that there was no obstacle in the way of her marriage save that of her youth? Could they not have waited, she and Peter? Then there would have been another wedding from the old house, and Dolores would have worn her great-grandmother's wedding veil, which was woven of dew and gossamer into a fine fall of yellowing lace. When were they coming home, these inconsiderate children? She and Cousin Sarah supposed they would live with Mr. Comstock.

Mr. Comstock supposed likewise. He wrote heavily to his son, in a spidery hand, ill-suited to the ponderous words. He was intensely displeased. Marriage was a state to be entered into solemnly. No good could come of anything so hasty, founded upon deceit and secrecy. But Peter and his wife were welcome to come home. He would give his son the same opportunity in the business that he would give any other young man—provided Peter would settle down, take life seriously, and work with all that was in him.

It never occurred to the women or to the old man to raise any legal quibble about the marriage. The couple was under age, yes. But to their guardians marriage was marriage, irrevocable.

Dolores answered her cousins. She was so happy, she wrote. Could they ever forgive her? No, they would not be coming home until later, on a visit, perhaps. Peter had his way to make in a world not his father's. Peter would be a great man, some day, and they would be proud of him. They would live in New York, and she would like to have her clothes and some of her own things, pictures, belongings. Later, she would write where to send them.

Peter wrote his father that they would not come home. He said he had not been happy in the mills, and never would be. He must be free . . . to write.

Ashabel Comstock did not answer that letter. The boy had made his bed, let him lie upon it. He locked the letter away, opened the great Bible with the cracking leather and the metal clasps. "I will arise and go to my father. . . ."

Desolate and bitter, the old man sat in the echoing library and read of a son who had repented.

The nest egg from the sale of Peter's automobile was fast melting. You can't live at hotels for nothing, they discovered. He had his own income, something over a hundred dollars a month; and Dolores had what was left of her "savings." Enough to go on, surely, they told each other gaily. Now they must get down to the business of life on the earth plane, they must leave the high hills and tender valleys behind them and set their faces toward the city.

Meadows drove up for them, fat and jocose. He'd seen

44

his uncle. Everything would be all right. Meantime, what were they living on, if he might be so bold?

Told, by Peter, he whistled. He was a generous youth with a large allowance. His hand went, metaphorically, to his pocket.

"Just a tide-over?"

"Not now . . . we'll manage . . . but . . . if I need anything . . . I'll remember. Thanks, old fellow."

Meadows was a fledgling broker in his father's firm. His dismissal from college had met with resignation at home. They had expected it, they said. He argued now, intensely, "Wall Street's the place, old egg. Where will you get to— on the *Star?*"

Peter explained . . . he must have work that would help him. He was going to write. He'd always meant to. Old Hodges understood that.

The cherubic face lengthened. Oh, of course, that bee still buzzing in his bonnet! Well, to town and an interview with the influential uncle, and meantimes Dolores could hunt for a place to live. Coralie, a good scout, would help her.

They reached town and at Meadows' insistence stayed with him in the paternal Park Avenue apartment. His people were absent, taking cures somewhere. Coralie came to a gay dinner, in a big dining room, and viewed the honeymooners with blonde cynicism. Her dimples and her giggles hid shrewdness. Meadows was "crazy about her." But she was waiting. If nothing better turned up . . . perhaps. . . . Nobody, he mourned, loves a fat man.

He paraded Peter downtown to the great offices of the *Star*. His uncle, Warren Mason, city editor of that sheet, sat behind a large, untidy desk and listened with despairing amusement to Peter's stammered ambitions. He'd seen so many of them, come and go. This one, a half-baked infant with eager speech and eyes was, he understood from Meadows, married. My God! Well, a cub reporter's job then . . . ?

Jubilant Peter returned to Park Avenue. He was . . . on a paper. He had visions of murder trials, of scoops. Oh, he'd make a name for himself, never fear; and nights, he'd write. He'd write the great play and the novel that teased him, the novel of freedom.

Coralie Young trotted a bewildered bride about town. She was amazed when she learned that Park Avenue was out of the question. Well, there was always lower Fifth or the Village. Furniture? They had none, nor could they buy any. After a day or two of hunting, east side first, then, a little scornfully, west side, Coralie came to the conclusion that she could do nothing for a pair of poverty-stricken lunatics. She told Hodge Meadows so.

"Nonsense, everybody lives somewhere!" he said.

Eventually they found something through an advertisement. It was excessively far uptown, a district as strange to Coralie as if it had been China. It was in a neighborhood screaming with rawness. Large blocks of dismal apartment houses stood there, planted and imperturbable. All the streets were not paved. Some were seas of spring mud, rutted and impossible. There were vacant lots, strewn with tin cans and refuse. And there were a hundred baby carriages dustily wheeling along the "Avenue." It was pretty bad.

The furnished apartment was that of a young couple who had heard of a "chance" in Florida. They were nice people, well washed and ungrammatical. They'd sublet cheap with the furniture and all, and the tenants could have the option of buying. The furniture was quite new, they said, and exhibited the overstuffed suite proudly. The rent, too, was from month to month, very satisfactory.

Feeling slightly sick, Dolores nodded, while Coralie sniffed about the rooms. Bedroom and parlor, all dark; great deal of golden oak, cubby hole bathroom and kitchen. But the place was clean. It would have to do.

Their landlords had only waited for tenants before they went southward in a battered flivver. In three days' time they moved out and Peter and Dolores moved in.

Peter had had a shock when he had learned something of the nature of his assignment, obscure weddings, funerals, very unimportant dinners. The sort of stuff they gave a raw girl to do on a paper. However, it wouldn't be long before he'd have front page, signed articles, he assured Dolores.

46

His hours were from three in the afternoon to midnight. Would she be afraid? He hadn't thought of "hours." He had expected to be free to write evenings. Never mind, he'd get up early and write mornings!

The house was new, badly built, the walls thin, the plaster already peeling. The clothes closets were slits in the wall. Dolores, used to space, found Peter always under her feet, when he was at home. There seemed so little room to turn.

"You'll really do your own work?" asked Coralie.

"Of course."

Coralie said something that might have been a prayer. Privately she thought them both mad, and Peter the madder of the two. What did he mean at his age and with his looks, tying himself down to this unworldly infant? She knew all about the mills. The situation was beyond her.

Dolores could cook, she had an instinct for housekeeping. But her practice had been confined to a dusting of treasures, the baking of a cake, the brewing of tea. She discovered she had much to learn as she struggled with a cookbook and a tiny gas stove. She burned her fingers, she grew hot and bedraggled in the airless kitchen. She learned the way to the nearest delicatessen.

Yet, at first, they were happy. It was a novelty if a rather disconcerting one, and they had each other.

Peter found his work more difficult than he had anticipated. Occasionally the desire to "show them" boiled over in the report of an uninteresting wedding. Blue pencils put a stop to that. Fine writing was not wanted he was told.

But he liked the atmosphere of the office, the noise and hurry, the smoke, the smell of paper and ink damp from the presses. He made friends, as always, easily. Certain timeworn practical jokes were played upon him, and he took them with good nature.

Now and then he brought some of his new comrades home, arriving after one o'clock. Dolores managed a meal somehow, and waited on them, flushed with her importance as "hostess." Her guests were favorably impressed. They sometimes said so in such frank terms as to embarrass her husband. They were consciously hard-boiled young men for the most part. Most of them were from other sections of the country. They wore terrible clothes and talked in many accents, smoked more than was good for them, argued, discussed, and were "cynical" into the dawn. And after a time Dolores would creep away and make ready for bed, feeling that the process was public, because of the thin walls and adjoining rooms. Much later, Peter would stumble in the darkness of the hot room where the windows stood open to summer, and yawning prodigiously, lie down beside her. Then she would wake, thinking drowsily of the dishes to be washed.

The nights were lonely before Peter came home. An even tempered young Norwegian woman who was her neighbor came in sometimes in the vast camaraderie of uptown. Now and then she would ask Dolores to "keep an ear out for Baby" while she and her husband went to the movies. "Baby" was fat and placid and not engaging. He afflicted Dolores with a sense of embarrassment and strangeness. He was not over clean and had none of the seraphic tricks one expected from babies. But she took her responsibility seriously and would often go to him and sit beside him if he cried or fretted. If she ever had a baby, that baby would be very different. It would have gray eyes like Peter's and dark hair like her own. But babies, Peter had explained to her, were out of the question . . . now.

Sometimes Peter telephoned that he'd been asked on a party. Did she mind? She wasn't afraid, was she, with Mrs. Oleson next door? And the lonely evening would drag by. She would get herself an unhealthy supper, wash up, try to read. But books had lost their interest for her. It was so still and hot in the flat. Now and then she ventured out for a walk, and once she went to a motion picture alone. But the picture was futile, the house hot and crowded and smelling of chewing gum and humanity, and a man spoke to her as she went in.

Peter would come home, excited and flushed with his "party." He'd been to a show, or he'd met so and so, or someone had pointed out someone else to him . . . you know, the columnist. Several times he drank too much and frightened her with thickened speech and unsteady steps. He was always sorry and headachy in the morning. But you couldn't sit in a fellow's flat all night, he explained, and keep awake and not drink.

The apartment irked them both, how much neither said. They were accustomed to different things. Ridiculous, that it should make a difference, silver and old china, and shining glass, and mahogany, as opposed to poor plate and coarse pottery, and thick tumblers, and golden oak or mission. But it did. If only, thought Dolores, I could have flowers. . . .

Occasionally Meadows motored up or 'phoned them to come down and do a theater or a roof garden with him and his crowd. Once twenty of them had a hilarious evening at Coney Island. But Meadows was not always in town. He took long week-ends and a longer vacation in the middle of the summer.

Yet the enchantment held. They were new to love, and to each other still. They could forget the cramped, stifling rooms, the noises, and the strangeness. They could be happy, walking in a kingdom of their own, west of the moon.

"You're not sorry?"

"Peter!"

"Darling, it won't always be like this. . . . I love you, Dolores, I adore you!"

"Kiss me," she would murmur, dreamily, "Peter . . . do you remember . . . ?"

And they would talk of the sea and a warm white beach, and the scent of summer over an old town. And they would pretend.

But you cannot always live west of the moon. There were dishes to wash and marketing to do, and the terrible city heat like a pall over them both. There were quarrels, about nothing. Tears, sometimes. Reproaches.

"*Must* you go out again?"

"I have to meet people, haven't I? How'll I get on otherwise? Masters is editor of the *Hermes*. If I could get in there . . . Dolores, don't you understand?"

49

She'd promised to leave him free, he thought, and even now, so soon, he felt her dragging at him, clipping his wings. If he'd been alone it would have been easy.

"Don't cry. I'm sorry. I didn't mean it. I love you."

CHAPTER VII

"LET's take young Comstock up to Felicity's," one of the young men in the city room suggested to another.

"Lord, must the Minotaur be fed?" asked his friend, grinning.

"Why not? She won't hurt him. There isn't an ounce of harm in the lady."

"Possibly not. She's simply a collector."

"How come?"

"Of youth. Really, she's done a lot of good—after a fashion. She never fastened her eye on me," lamented Simpson, "I wasn't born young enough. She likes 'em with the dew of ideals fresh upon them. Budding genius for choice. Well, possibly Comstock's that. He *says* so, at any rate."

The perpetrator of this artless prank, one Bill Gaines, sought out Peter.

"Ever hear of Felicity Hawthorne?" he asked solemnly.

Peter's gray eyes, tired eyes now, widened.

"Yes. And of Mr. Coolidge too," he answered gently.

"Glad you're so well informed. Want to meet her?"

"Being funny, aren't you?" asked Peter who had seen the lady twice, from the other side of the footlights.

"Not very. She gives Sunday afternoon parties. Tea and talk. She would be good for you to know. She's made more than one playwright in her day."

He named a rendezvous and an early hour and sauntered off. Peter went out upon a dull assignment trying to

51

control his mounting excitement. He was working hard on his play, a rough draft was ready. Felicity Hawthorne—how her name sang!—was the ideal type for his gallant, misunderstood *Mona*. If he could only arouse her interest! Wait until he told Dolores!

Dolores was slow to grasp the idea of the golden opportunity.

"I thought . . . one went to a manager with plays?"

"Not always. Miss Hawthorne has all the influence in the world. She practically selects her own things, you know. Oh, Dolores, it's such a wonderful chance!"

"I wish I could go too. . . ."

"You must meet her, of course," promised Peter, absently, "but this first time . . . Heavens . . . how many days . . . four? An eternity! I'll work like a nailer until then."

He had sold a few things, a thumbnail sketch and some light verse. He had the plot of his novel down on paper. But somehow he couldn't seem to get at anything for long. The atmosphere of the flat was not conducive to unbroken work. There were constant interruptions. Dolores, trying so hard to be quiet, would often break in upon him. The ice-man would come. The telephone might ring . . . generally a mistake. The next door baby was teething. There were days when it cried constantly in a thin rebellious wail which seemed to pierce through the fragile lace work of his careful sentences like an arrow. Oh for quiet! A log camp in the woods, or even his old room at home!

Sunday came and Peter paid careful attention to his sartorial preparations. He was fussy about his tie. There was a hole in the best pair of silk socks. Would Dolores mend it for him?

Dolores, a little pale and drawn from the heat, would, and did. Why was Miss Hawthorne in town, she wondered?

Peter replied that he believed her new play would go into rehearsal shortly. Gaines said she was only in the city occasionally. She had a place on Long Island, but kept her flat open. Married? Oh, he believed so, to a doctor.

How old? He hadn't any idea, she looked about twenty but must be, of course, ten years older than that.

"Oh, *quite* old then," commented Dolores conscious of relief.

When he was ready she asked:

"I forgot to tell you. That girl Hodge brought up here once—Lucie—something-or-other. She telephoned. She is having a tea to-day and wants me to come. Is it all right?"

"Why not? Have you car-fare, darling? Hope you have a good time."

She called, as he was leaving:

"When will you be home?"

"Late, of course. I'm stealing the time as it is."

He expressed a slight irritation as he ran blithely down the three flights of "marble" steps. When would he be home? And was it "all right" for Dolores to go out? How absurd, in the face of their bargain. Well, she did her best. She was a darling, the dearest in the world.

Alone, Dolores jerked an impatient hand over her eyes. Why did they persist in filling with tears? She went to the disordered bedroom and began to hunt her clothes in the cramped closet. She hadn't liked Lucie very much. She understood from Hodge that she was a "good scout"; that she "worked" in a village tea room.

Presently she was ready and started on the long trip downtown. It didn't matter if she came home late. There were cold things in the ice-box and heaven alone knew when Peter would return.

Liking Lucie or not, the expedition had the charm of the unusual. She wondered, wistfully, in the subway, if she'd meet someone she could really like. A girl, a friend. She hadn't minded not making intimate friends at home. She hadn't missed them. She'd had her books and Peter. Well, she still had them but it appeared that they weren't enough.

Peter found Miss Hawthorne surrounded by what looked like a mob scene. Her apartment in the east fifties, by the river, was all vague colorings and dimness. She herself was as pretty as porcelain and as soft as silk. Peter was presented with mock solemnity.

53

"A coming Eugene O'Neill, Miss Hawthorne."

Felicity fluttered about him. She had great blue eyes and authentically golden hair, and an elfin figure. She talked in italics. She was *so glad to* meet Mr. Comstock . . . which was true. She had heard *so* much about him—which was a fib.

She made a place for him beside her tea table and poured with a dainty clashing of cups and silver, and a hovering Japanese servant at her side. Felicity did not serve cocktails. She was opposed to all the blatant things of life, jazz and flasks, and uproarious dancing. She liked to sit quietly in her long, hushed drawing-room and contemplate her white hands or her listeners' admiring eyes and talk about the state of the drama and her soul. Only the young took her seriously. But she had her place in the stage world. She possessed unusual charm. She was thirty-three years old and would go on playing innocent, misunderstood heroines until her neckline or her delicate skin failed her. There had been a time when she had surrounded herself with what were then known as "older men." Now she preferred her satellites under twenty, if possible, and preferred them to be talented. She adored the role of strictly moral Egeria. And her husband, who was a very great surgeon, smiled at her preferences as a man smiles at a child at its play, its destructive hands among the fragile toys. He had long since learned to believe that she had sentiment and no passion, and he realized that what heart she had was given to himself. If he pitied her "circle" he never said so.

The young men drifted in and out. The shadows grew. The Japanese moved soundlessly, rosy lights sprang up, there was a heavy scent of flowers.

"I want to hear *all* about your play—you *must* come sometime to Centrebrook for a week-end and read me what you have. You will like it there, the water is like jasper and the sky like lapis," she said, gently.

Peter looked at her with hunger for beauty and far things in his eyes. She seemed the merest girl, sitting there, her feet in their strapped shoes crossed, her hands folded on the pale tints of her gown. She had sad eyes, he thought,

54

and a pink, unpomaded mouth, wistfully heartshaped. And her voice was like little bells ringing or muted notes on a violin. He wondered about her husband. Doubtless, he treated her badly! Peter pictured him as old and crass and brutal, a portrait which would have amused Doctor Van Anden, just now returning from the hospital, his fine leonine head against the cushions of his ear, his sensitive face relaxed into lines of weariness. He was hoping—and knowing the hope futile—that Felicity would be rid of her youngsters by now, and would give him tea, and perhaps sing to him in the golden summer dusk, her small lovely voice sliding dreamily through the room. Well, one day she would tire of her dolls, he thought, as he fiitted a latch key to his door, looked at the conglomeration of hats and sticks in the hall, raised an eyebrow whimsically and departed for his private quarters. For when she tired he would leave the hospital scents and sounds behind him and they would go abroad and live their lives out in a garden.

His wife, he reflected, was a shallow woman. But shallows hold so much sunshine, they reflect such charming things. She couldn't help her hunger for admiration. And he loved her.

When Peter reached home he looked with an increased distaste at golden oak and "overstuffed." He hadn't realized how much he'd miss beautiful things. Even in his own house the furniture had, he thought for the first time, a beauty of its own, solidity, the polish of tradition. The sort of things among which he and Dolores now lived would never lose that raw look, that paid-out-of-income appearance, that department store veneer.

He went into his bedroom and woke Dolores from a restless sleep. He sat down on the bed and she sat up and looked at him. He was a Peter returned to her, a Peter whom she had missed these last weeks. His gray eyes shone and his mouth was curved to laughter.

"It was great!" he told her, like a small boy, "and she's wonderful. She wants to read the play. She wants me to come out to Long Island with it soon and read her every word. She promised to help me."

"Out to Long Island—without me?" asked Dolores, not quite awake.

"Oh, but, *darling!*"

He looked at her with a quaint annoyance. Dolores asked:

"You didn't say you were married?"

"No, of course not. One doesn't, you know. Just out with it—plump, 'By the way, did you know I was married!' Don't be absurd, dear. This is business . . . opportunity."

As she still looked at him, wonderingly, dark eyes heavy with sleep, he burst out impatiently:

"Don't you understand? You're trying to *make* us—so *married!*"

His impulsive gesture, brushing aside old conventions and standards, brought back to her that other Peter who had preached freedom to her, who had converted her, with whom she had run away to find—what? She said low:

"I'm sorry."

He rose, undressed, talking all the while. Later lying beside her, still trying to tell her how marvellous the day had been, how much he hoped from this inspiring contact, he found that she had fallen asleep, and was breathing quietly like a child. He broke off in mid-sentence, scowling into the darkness. What had marriage done to Dolores? She had always been so ready to listen, her heart had run to his on eager feet, she had encouraged him with her eyes and her mobile face, and hands, and her exclamations. Now she was always too tired. She was just a wife, he thought savagely, her thoughts always elsewhere, on the dull happenings of the duller day. She no longer went side by side with him into his world of dreams.

In the morning before settling to work he remembered to ask rather perfunctorily:

"Did you have a good time at your tea yesterday?"

She came to his side, by the hideous desk, a blue apron tied around her slim waist, her hands reddened and spongy from dishwater. A lock of hair fell into her eyes, she brushed it back wearily. She'd have it bobbed, she thought, as the other girls had. But Peter had always liked it long,

56

he'd loved to see it down at night and to watch the slow sweep and turn of her brush through its darkness.

"Yes. . . ."

She sat down beside him while he handled his papers impatiently and shifted the carriage of the rented typewriter.

"The tea room was awfully funny—all peacocks painted on a whitewashed wall. Lucie was nice to me. She's not very young, she must be twenty-five. Her aunt was there, a Miss Karsten, who owns the shop. I liked her. She—Peter —she asked me if I wanted to go to work there—they are short a girl."

He looked at her in astonishment.

"Work . . . ? There? In a Village tea room? I never heard such nonsense!"

"But, Peter, I'd like it. There would be . . . wages . . . and tips, perhaps. And it would be fun."

"It's out of the question," he told her firmly, and put a sheet of paper into the jaws of the waiting machine.

"But why not? I've nothing to do? You know—we said —I was to find a job. . . ."

"That was different," said Peter, amazingly. "We weren't married then!"

He added, to himself—"nor were we planning to be."

Dolores said, puzzled:

"I don't see the difference. It's hard to get along on what we have. I wanted to help, you know, not to hinder."

"Well, you can't and that's that," he said shortly and turned to his work.

Peter Comstock's wife serving in a tea room! It was unthinkable!

Dolores rose. She stood beside him, irresolute.

"But—we were to leave each other free!"

"You're free enough," he answered, turning to face her, his eyes estranged. "But I won't have you taking ridiculous jobs in absurd places. I can support you. I married you with that intention."

"But—but when we thought we weren't to be married, Peter?"

He replied angrily, raising his voice:

"That put things on a different basis. We *did* get married, didn't we? Well, as long as we stay married you'll please not try and run things for us."

He turned to the machine and smote out an incoherent sentence or two. Dolores walked away, stopped, said doubtfully:

"But Peter . . ."

"Oh, damn it!" he shouted, "can't you see I want to work? Can't you leave me alone!"

She went into the bedroom and slammed the door, hard. Mrs. Oleson, next door, bathing the baby, looked at the shaken wall and smiled wearily. She knew the symptoms.

Dolores cast herself on the bed and stormily wept. He'd sworn at her! He'd looked at her as though he'd hated her! As though it had been her fault! As though she'd forced him into marriage!

Why should he be "free" to go off visiting actresses, she asked herself childishly, and why should she be bound to coop herself up in this hideous place? It wasn't fair!

"As long as we stay married," Peter had said.

CHAPTER VIII

"ROAD'S END LODGE," Felicity Hawthorne's place at Centrebrook, Long Island, was an amazing structure. It had been Dr. Van Anden's wedding gift. That is to say, he remarked, "Pick your site and your architect and go ahead." She brought the plans to him in some perturbation of spirit, the youthful architect hovering in the background. Van Anden had laughed. "What am I to make of these things?" he asked, with a gesture toward the blue prints. "Get on with it, Felicity, and remember to save me a few feet of floor space wherein I can be quiet."

When the house was completed its official master gazed at it in a sort of tender amusement.

"It is incredible," he murmured to his wife. "It is absurd and adorable . . . just like you."

And it was.

The house stood on a miniature cliff overlooking the Sound.

It was constructed of field stone, and had a roof of simulated thatch which jutted out like eyebrows. The entire building rambled, curved and made discreet, retiring gestures. It was a house in a fairy story. It had guarding cedars, leaning to the wind, and a sheltered enclosure held tiny Japanese garden iris, cherry and coaxed, exotic blooms, with a rustic bridge over an artificial pool, and summer houses built like pagodas.

Peter Comstock saw the house first on a warm day in September. He had been twice to call upon Felicity in town, the last time he had found her comparatively alone —not more than six people were in the room—and she had set a definite date. There was some hitch in her rehearsals. She could afford to take a few days' holiday. Peter got leave and Dolores packed a bag for him with red lips set.

"You're not sending me off in the best of spirits," he told her.

"I know. I'm sorry. I'm . . . jealous!"

He looked at her, amazed, and laughed:

"Jealous? You? Of Miss Hawthorne? Come, Dolores, it isn't in you to be so foolish and mistaken."

"Oh, not of her . . . but of the things that take you from me, that I can't share."

"You wouldn't stand in my light?" he asked her, gently. "It will mean so much to me if I can interest her in the play."

"I know. I'm a wretch."

When he had gone she looked forlornly about the flat. Oh, oh, in theory how easy it had sounded! Freedom for man and wife. Come and go at will, no questions asked. The right to an individual life to possess your own self wholly, to make your own contacts.

In practice it was harder. She told herself fiercely that if Peter insisted upon her living up to her compact he hadn't lived up to his. What rights did she have in this ménage? She looked scornfully at the rickety bookcase overflowing with their brave, loud-shouting books. How much did the authors know when they preached their world-shaking doctrines?

At Road's End Lodge Peter spent two bewildered days. The place was tumultuous with guests, reporters, photographers. Meals were continuous—people roamed in and out. The place was like a well ordered madhouse in a dream. And through it all Felicity Hawthorne wandered graciously. She greeted her guests when they arrived and forgot them until they were forced upon her attention. During the two days Peter had half an hour alone with her in the garden, walking across the intricate ridiculous bridge, sitting in the pagoda, watching goldfish gleam idly in water which was a bright, unchanging blue from the coloring of the cement lining the pool.

He poured out, breathless and stirred, the main idea of his play. She listened and her eyes kindled.

"You must read it to me!" she said, and forgot she had said it before.

"I have it here. . . ."

"Not yet. There are too many people. I am distracted just now. My new piece will not do at all. Something else must be found. Your play? Why not? We will see. Come down again, we shall work on it together."

Doctor Van Anden appeared briefly. Peter's imaginative soul was shocked upon meeting him. His unflattering portrait of Felicity's husband was at once dispelled. Van Anden was very pleasant to him. He confided:

"When I can't stand the crowds any longer I go to Southampton and scare up an operation. There's peace in an operating room, you know," and he laughed at Peter with kind and cynical eyes.

When Peter reached home Dolores was impatient to hear his news. She had made up her mind to regain his confidence.

"Did she read it? What did she say?"

"There was no time. A lot of other people were there. We talked about it, and she promised to work on it with me."

"But I thought . . ."

"You don't understand. How could she give me all her time? Harrod, the English novelist, was visiting, her manager came down for lunch, she had other important people."

He was brusque, and unamiable. He did not want to discuss Felicity Hawthorne with Dolores. It would be like rhapsodizing over the spring. He was not in the slightest degree in love with her, in the accepted term of the phrase. He was, there being no other word for it, enchanted. She seemed like a creature from another world, a little more than mortal. And in her expressive hands she held the power after which he panted.

As summer's end slipped golden and blue into autumn

he went again to Road's End Lodge, and yet again. On the third occasion he read his play to Felicity. She listened, aloof, frowning slightly. When the last sheets of manuscript dropped from his lean fingers and he leaned toward her, eager as a child for a word of approbation, she said slowly, in her tender voice:

"It has possibilities. *Mona* could be made a marvelous character. My friend, as yet you know very little about women."

"I suppose not," he murmured abashed, remembering that he had never told her of his marriage.

"I can help you. I'm going back to town. We have shelved my play and I shal wait until the right vehicle is found. In the meantime, I shall have more leisure. We can work on your play together."

"I can't thank you enough. . . ."

"Don't try." She smiled, dim rose and pearl. "When you are a great man I shall have received my reward."

To Dolores he explained, briefly:

"Miss Hawthorne is going to help me with the play. What time I can spare, I'll be with her."

Dolores felt as if she had been struck in the face. There was a time when she had been the helper, when every word of dialogue, every bit of business had been discussed with her. Not that she knew anything about the art of carpentering a play and, she admitted freely, no doubt Miss Hawthorne *did* know, but Peter had sworn to her that she was invaluable to him . . . as an inspiration. That was before they were married.

If they had not married . . . ? If she'd been brave enough?

Marriage was terrible, she thought, desolately. It changed you so.

Peter was relieved from the unimportant social items and given police court news to cover, a little more exciting and surely better. Occasionally he came home stirred over some incident, tragic or humorous. He had a notebook full. He was still kept in rigid bounds by the austere blue pencil, but Mason was gruffly pleased with him—his salary was raised. It was a longer road to the front page than he anticipated. Still, he would get there.

He was home very little. His working hours were uncertain, and his free time devoted to Felicity, dependent on her whim. She was as good as her word. She worked with him in her sedate library where a vibrant fire of cedar logs burned, the fragrance mingling with that of heavy headed roses. She tore his play to pieces and bade him put them together again. He was quick to see that she knew the mechanics, that her drama sense was unerring, but was disappointed, although he would not acknowledge it to himself, in her lapses into banality. She would rewrite a line he had thought subtle and clap her hands childishly at the result. "That's what you meant, wasn't it, Peterkin?" But it was not, very often.

Sometimes she would tire and push the scribbled manuscript from her.

"No more to-day . . . talk to me."

But it would be she who talked, gently, always of herself.

Her cousins wrote Dolores, "Why haven't you and Peter come home?" And she answered, gallantly . . . they were too busy. Peter was doing so well, yes, she was much occupied, she had many friends. . . .

Lies, the last excuse. But why shouldn't she make it truth, she asked. Why shouldn't she have friends—be occupied?

The teashop and Miss Karsten's offer stayed in her memory. Why not? Peter would say no, of course. But need she tell him? She had so much time. He was home so rarely, and so late. He needn't know.

So she went down to 8th Street and confronted the tall, raw-boned woman who wore eccentric clothes smartly, and had the coin-clear head of a young, feminine Viking.

"Could you give me work?"

"I could," said Asta Karsten briskly.

Dolores was sick with embarrassment.

"I have to explain. . . . I'm not so sure about hours . . . you see, my husband. . . ."

"Ridiculous that you should have one. Well, what about him?"

"He wouldn't . . . approve. . . ."

Asta stared at her.

"In this age? You've married an antique—should be in a glass case, I'd say."

"I'm so alone," Dolores burst out, "all day, mostly—and sometimes all night. This newspaper business—and his writing. Miss Karsten, if I don't do something I'll go mad."

Asta Karsten nodded abruptly.

"I know. I lived through it . . . twice. Never say once bitten, twice shy. I was a fool. The first was a writer, the second an actor. Never again. We're busy enough here. I can give you part time, whatever hours you can come. How about tea and dinner . . . ? Could you manage?"

She could. At first it was very strange, but she grew to like it, the smoke and talk, the Villagers who sat for hours wrangling at little tables, the Park Avenue people who drifted in with an air of slumming, the smell of good coffee and the Norwegian cakes for which Miss Karsten's place was known.

It was not hard to deceive Peter. He never asked her where she had been or what she had been doing. On the rare occasions when he came home early and she was not there he accepted a stammered explanation without comment.

Christmas came. She'd planned a tiny tree and some gifts bought from what was proudly "her own money." Peter was charming. He squandered savings on a little moonstone ring to guard the Port Chester wedding ring, or rather to replace it, for she rarely wore it, now.

It was a happy evening. But he left her before midnight. He had promised to look in upon Felicity, she was having a few friends, her manager would be there.

Shortly after this he found out about the tea room.

One of the reporters who had been Dolores' guest on the early scratch-supper parties "happened in" and saw her. He said to Peter, stopping by his desk:

"Tell your wife she should always wear orange smocks."

"What on earth do you mean?"

"I saw her at Peacock Feathers . . . how long has she been working there?"

Peter replied, indifferently:

"Not very long."

He went home, breaking an engagement with Felicity. He was in a cold rage. Lie to him, would she, make him a laughing stock?

She wasn't home. He waited, fretting, trying to write, fighting with his typewriter. When the shift key stuck he raised the entire machine and crashed it down on the desk. The method worked but could not be recommended. The flat looked undusted, cheerless, the janitor was not generous with heat. There were unwashed dishes in the sink. . . .

She came in about ten o'clock. A cold wind had whipped color in her face, she was smiling, she'd had an entertaining day.

Peter sat there, the desk strewn with cigarette butts. He did not rise, but regarded her gloomily.

"Where have you been?"

She had her hands raised to pull off her hat. It hurt her a little . . . she had so much hair, and hats were made for the shingled.

"I . . . I . . ."

"Oh, don't bother to lie. I'll have you the trouble of drawing on your imagination. You're working down at that tea-room place. How long?"

Her knees felt weak. She sat down, trembling and told him.

"I see. And it was so unimportant that you felt it wouldn't interest me?"

"I don't see why I shouldn't lead my own life!" she cried out at him.

"I told you I wouldn't have you down there. I know that crowd. Shallow, silly and—vicious, some of them. I suppose you've made friends? Men friends?"

"No."

"You expect me to believe you? You expect me to believe you ever again?"

"But *why* are you so angry, Peter?" she called out in despair. "It is all so harmless. I had to have something to fill up my time."

"You have your home."

She looked around at it. Her lovely mouth hardened.

"Home? *This place?*"

"Well?"

"It . . . it can't occupy me," she told him, "and you're away all the time . . . with that woman. . . ."

"Leave her out of it. My God, do you want to tie me down like a grocery clerk? Do you want me to stay home and wash the dishes and read the newspaper in the evening, and fall asleep in my chair at nine o'clock?"

"No, I don't. I want you to make your way. But it's no reason why I shouldn't make mine too—why I shouldn't have my work."

"Your *work?* Handing coffee cups to Village sheiks?"

"Peter!"

But he had to grow dramatic.

"Taking tips, too!" he said. "The prettier the smile, the bigger the tip. My wife!"

"But don't you see," she cried eagerly, "that's just the point. Before we were married . . . when . . . when . . . we had other plans, it was understood that I should work, and have my chance to prove myself a wage earner; that you wouldn't stand in my way any more than I'd stand in yours."

He said:

"You bear my name now. I'm responsible for you."

"What difference does the name make? Hundreds of married women don't use their husbands' names. Marrying you a thousand times over doesn't make me any less Dolores Brewster than I was, does it?"

"You're Dolores Comstock," he told her doggedly. "If you were not my wife you'd be free enough to do as you pleased. I'd have nothing to say. I wouldn't want to. But as long as you are my wife I won't have you working in dubious shops and having people say that I can't support you."

"Peter," she whispered, "you *can't!*"

66

He looked at her, bewildered:

"I . . . can't?" he repeated stupidly.

"No. Not the way I . . . I tell you I hate this place," she cried out. "It's like a prison. It stifles me."

"And you think," he asked with a deadly courtesy, "that you can so increase my poor earnings that we'll be able to move into more suitable surroundings?"

"Oh, don't take that tone . . . of course not, now . . . I . . . I don't want to be in a tea shop forever."

"What else can you do?"

She said, defiantly:

"Asta says I could go on the stage. . . ."

"Asta?"

"Miss Karsten."

He leaned back in his chair and laughed.

"Stage? You? Do you think I'd permit it?"

"How could you stop me?"

"You're my wife!" he repeated, and as she stared at him across this gulf that had opened up between them he said, tempestuously, without thinking, "I . . . accepted the responsibility, Dolores . . . you . . . forced it on me, you know."

She looked at him, wildly, voicelessly. Then she rose and ran from the room. He heard the bedroom door slam, the key turn. He heard the springs of the bed creak as she cast her full weight upon them. He heard her uncontrolled sobbing, the weeping of an angry child.

He rose, went toward the door and halted. Then, with the gesture of tension at the snapping point, he snatched his hat from the antlered rack and left the apartment.

CHAPTER IX

Snow blew in gusts and eddies over the vacant lots. The bleak houses seemed to shrink into themselves. The walls admitted the voice of the complaining wind in every room.

Since their quarrel Dolores and Peter had been on the most formal terms. They were regretful, they said, but Peter's apology was hardly whole-hearted.

"I'm sorry I was quick tempered. I shouldn't have put things that way."

Dolores had written a note to Asta Karsten pleading illness. She was unable to swallow her pride and go to 8th Street and say, humbly, "I couldn't carry it through. He won't let me work here any longer."

She wondered if, resigning herself to Peter's ultimatum, he would be more considerate of her, stay at home, take her into his confidence. To her amazement and anger he made no comment when it became obvious that she was no longer going down to the tea shop. He seemed to take it for granted.

Women in shabby furs and clumsy arctics jostled against her in the markets where she bought her provisions. She saw youth without beauty, and the pinched look of genteel poverty. The children had chapped hands and red little noses, needing attention. Half grown boys slithered across her tracks on sleds, threw snowballs. The days were dark, almost all day long the electric light burned in the flat. A card from Hodge Meadows' friend Coralie reached her.

68

Coralie was at Palm Beach . . . the weather, she said in purple ink, was wonderful.

Next door Mrs. Oleson's baby died of influenza. There was no privacy in the cardboard apartments. Dolores, sitting alone during the baby's brief illness, heard the hurried steps of the mother, the hoarse crying of the child; heard the doctor come and go; heard, eventually, the sudden hush; the noisy grief, the inarticulate animal rebellion. She went next door to see what she could do, simply because she could not sit still, trembling, nauseated, and listen.

Mrs. Oleson, her eyes inflamed, her blonde hair straggling, took her coming as a matter of course. Other neighbors came too, all did what they could.

When the baby had been buried Dolores sat in the living room and turned over some of Peter's manuscript with Felicity's notations upon it and began to read, out of sheer desperation. Recently, he had not read her a word of the rapidly shaping play. Now she read it for herself.

It seemed to her that the character of *Mona* was no longer as Peter had planned it. The early *Mona* had been a gallant creature, fighting for freedom and individuality, refusing to be crushed by the marriage machine. The puppet which had evolved itself under Felicity's guidance was a soft, appealing woman, uttering banal phrases, moving about the stage with consciously dramatic effect. The character of the husband, which had been created equal, resolved itself into a background for *Mona*.

Dolores pushed the sheets from her. She had an acute, if untutored, literary sense, she felt the play "good theater" and no more. It was no longer what Peter had meant it to be—a demand for liberty, and comradeship and sharing between man and wife. It had become a commonplace drama, crammed with sugar-coated sex.

She told herself reluctantly, he's lost the spark.

Finally, she went back to 8th Street and resumed her duties. Miss Karsten viewed her shrewdly from frosty blue eyes and asked no questions. She was glad to have her back for Dolores was popular. She was deft and decorative. She had the look of race and a voice which could repeat an order for cakes and coffee and make music of it. Someday, thought Miss Karsten, who was nothing if not foresighted, the girl would wake up and would find that the world lay at her feet.

There were men who dropped in, asked her to sit at their tables, and made excuses to talk to her. When she was embarrassed, which was often, she had a soft delicious stammer which they found charming.

Peter was slow in realizing that she had returned to the work he prohibited. When he taxed her with it she looked at him with hostile eyes.

"What are you going to do about it?" she asked him.

He was staggered. What could he do? "I forbid" were two idle words. After all he couldn't chain her, or lock her up.

She was now eighteen. The letter from the trustees reached her—she came into her small income. She showed the letter to Peter.

"We might afford to move?" she suggested tentatively.

He frowned, tossed the letter aside.

"It's yours. Spend it as you wish. I'll take care of the household. I won't live on your money," he told her brusquely.

She folded up the letter and went into the bedroom. Share and share alike?

Peter finished his play and had it typed at great expense, but the pretty blue binding gave it an official look and fostered the idea that he had created something orderly out of chaos. He took the product to Felicity, who was again in rehearsals.

"It's done."

She looked at him, smiled wistfully.

"I'm sorry. It's been fun, hasn't it?"

"More than that. . . ."

She liked the worshipful look in his eyes. She basked in it like a cat sunning herself.

"I'll give you some letters," she said, fumbling in her desk for her monogrammed paper, picking up her powder blue quill pen.

"But," he stammered at a loss, "for yourself? Your own manager?"

"My dear boy, we've taken on this thing of Merritt's. It would be two seasons before I am free. Meantime you should get it placed if possible."

"But the part . . . is *yours*."

She was tiring of him. She tired quickly. There was a new interest impending, a blond young poet whom someone or other had dug up for her. He had already had a slender success. Her name would certainly stand on the dedication page of his next volume.

"My part? Oh, I don't think so. I haven't, all along. It's too heavy for me, Peter, I need lightness, humor. . . ."

She looked at his despairing face and relented suddenly. After all, he had talent. How much, she did not know. It was possible that one day he might make something of himself and she would like to have had a hand in it. She said quickly:

"This is only your first attempt, you know. I do think you will place it. I'll do my best. I have been wondering . . . after I am through with Merritt's play . . . how about a comedy? Would you care to try it? I'd help you. Something light and sparkling and sophisticated, but with an undercurrent of poetry."

Her dreaming eyes, her quietly smiling face, fired him, as usual. He was ready to fling his work into the fire and to begin again. He left her, stuttering as many thanks as if she'd stood over him while he'd signed a contract.

He began the round of managers, armed with her letters, but the managers were wary. One of the minor things that annoyed the fraternity was Felicity's generosity in weaponing young, good-looking playwrights with gracious notes, "This will introduce my very good friend Mr. So-and-So . . . very talented . . . please do what you can for him."

The play was tossed about from office to office, sometimes it was read and sometimes it was not.

Meantime the work on the *Star* went on, the difficult hours, the assignments that took him all over the city. Police court work was too palling. The front page seemed further off then ever. Now and then he produced what he felt to be a human-interest story, and Mason read it with a kindly snort. It rarely found space.

Life resolved itself into a dull round of noise and headaches, of snatching meals anywhere, of coming home to a cheerless flat that was as often as not empty.

But he went to work on the comedy. He would not be beaten. He worked feverishly, without inspiration other than the burning desire to succeed. Dolores watched him.

"You're killing yourself. . . ."

"No. . . ."

"Tell me what it is to be about."

It hurt her to have to ask. At first he ignored the demand, later, in a blind groping for understanding, he told her as much as he had worked out, and waited her verdict with something of the old shining in his eyes.

"Well?"

"But its cheap . . . Peter, and obvious."

"What do you mean . . . cheap?"

"Perhaps not that," she contradicted herself hurriedly, "perhaps I mean manufactured . . . there doesn't seem to be any reality in it."

"It's not a drama," he said angrily, "nor a piece of realism. It's sheer comedy."

"But can't that be real? Laughter is."

"You don't understand." After a silence he flung out, angrily, "Miss Hawthorne thinks I'll make a go of it."

"Does she? Are you sure? Sure she isn't just playing with you, Peter? I've heard things about her."

"Well, don't repeat them to *me*, please!"

"Oh, Peter, not bad. . . . I didn't mean that. But she isn't doing you any good, dear. She's draining your strength. She's a . . . a . . . I hate the word, but I mean it, she's like a vampire. . . ."

"What nonsense!"

He turned back to his work, he had forgotten her.

They still had their hours of tenderness together, their hours of young, idyllic passion. They loved and they had youth. But the hours were growing less. It is hard to be tender when every nerve in your body is frayed by a petty accumulation of irritations. It is difficult to lose yourself in ardor when you are tired and bewildered, and things have gone wrong all day. Sometimes their embraces were mere attempts at escape from themselves, and, paradoxically, from each other.

Felicity's new play was produced. She sent seats to Peter and he took Dolores, and they watched the unfolding of the story—a light, amusing thing with a note of wistfulness which she dominated, moving through the business and the speeches aloofly, charmingly, with that air of dreaming innocence, that freedom from conscious sex-appeal which was stronger than any blatant flaunting of her enchantment would be. The play was like a dim veil cast about her white, slender body, through its swathing one had glimpses, alluring and unsatisfying, of the woman.

If Dolores had not been jealous of Felicity Hawthorne before she was now. She apeared gross to herself, too healthy, too much flesh and blood. That other woman had subtlety.

The critics, next morning, were not very kind. The public, they said, was tiring of innocence and wistfulness as a yearly occurrence. The tenuous charm of this well known actress was beginning to fray, to wear thin in spots. Wasn't it time that she played a real woman . . . if she could?

Peter was hot with indignation. He tossed the papers to Dolores, wondered if by any chance he might be able to catch the *Star* critic unaware and knock him down. As the *Star* critic weighed two hundred pounds and was a passionate amateur boxer the chance was meager.

"What a lot of fools!"

"But they're right!" said Dolores.

"Oh, of course! You would say so!"

He flung himself out of the room. She sat quite still. She couldn't say "It was intelligent criticism on my part, not jealousy." For some of it was jealousy.

Peter went to see Miss Hawthorne as soon as he could, stealing half an hour to tell her what asses all dramatic critics were. But Miss Hawthorne denied herself to everyone—except her husband. It was not the first time in recent years that the morning after had been unkind to

73

her. Van Anden knew how to handle her in these moods of petulant and bewildered hurt.

"Oh, come, what do they matter . . . this pack of mercenaries? Look at the box office instead . . . you have your following, you have your own public, it won't be turned aside by a smart-alec paragraph in a paper."

"But my art . . . my art!"

He kissed her, held her in his arms.

"Your art is always uniquely your own. No one else can touch you. Come, dry your eyes, play for all you are worth to-night. You're safe. And when you are tired of all this pretty posturing I'll take you away somewhere and you shall live like a Dresden shepardess in an old-world garden with a thousand roses all about you, and watch-dog of a husband to come to heel at a whistle."

So she ceased to cry, dried her eyes and rang for tea, and was quite happy for an hour. No one really counted for her emotionally except Van Anden. The others, the circle of boys, they were simply mirrors in which she saw herself reflected, gracious, inspirational and remote. With Van Anden she was a spoiled child, a charming toy, a rosy infant to be kissed and cosseted.

One night Peter returned home earlier than usual. There was a note on the maple syrup varnish of the dresser.

"I'm staying at the shop late. Miss Karsten is having a party after closing time. I 'phoned the office but didn't get you. Couldn't you come down?"

His first impulse was to go. His second, which he obeyed, was to stay at home and wait.

She came in at after two in the morning. There had been dancing and her cheeks were still flushed with it. Under her orange work smock she had worn a silver dress, one of her Boston dresses, almost new for she wore it so rarely. She came in happily.

"Peter . . . such a good time! Such interesting people! I kept watching the door for you!"

He said, stonily:

"Sit down—we'll have this out. . . ."

She slipped off her heavy coat, pulled off the long-sleeved smock, sat down, and smoothed her silver ruffles.

His tone disturbed her, drove back her happy mood upon itself.

"You're not angry, Peter?"

"Angry?" he laughed shortly. "Angry, when my wife comes home at three in the morning after carousing with a lot of loose people!"

"Peter!"

"I mean it!"

He stood up, very tall, and over-slender. Color burned in his cheeks, his hair was tossed.

"You'll cut it out, do you hear me? You'll stop going to that damned place. You'll stay home and behave yourself!"

Now she rose to face him. They were children, quarrelling. Ten years back they would have scratched and slapped and bitten like angry kittens.

"I will not. I'll do as I please. You can't stop me!"

"Can't I . . . ?"

He seized her wrist, pulled her closer to him, looked furiously at the beautiful oval of her face, the shaken scarlet of her mouth. A sudden passion overtook him. He held her close and kissed her again and again as she twisted and cried out in his embrace. His eyes had not softened, and his kisses were like blows.

Presently he let her go. She staggered, fell against the carven arm of the couch, supported herself there, her face white, save where kisses had marked it.

"You'd do that to me! While you were angry! While you were *hating* me!"

He said, sullenly:

"I do as I please with you. You're my wife."

After a long moment she said, childishly:

"I wish I weren't. I hate being your wife. I *hate* it!"

With the nervous gesture of rage mingled with another, and no finer emotion, he swept everything under his hand from the desk. A bottle of ink fell, rolled over, spilled out its thick clogged black on the rented carpet. Neither of them noticed.

"You know what you can do!" he said.

She picked up her coat and huddled it about her. She was trembling and very cold.

"Listen to me," she said trying to steady her voice. "Let's not . . . scream and shout. . . ."

"I'm not shouting!"

She put her hands to her ears.

"We'll—get free somehow," she told him. "This marriage—it's all been a mistake."

He looked at her a moment in silence. The anger and the passion departed. He echoed, dully . . . "a mistake. . . ."

When the word had been said they looked at each other and were frightened and lonely.

CHAPTER X

PETER woke to a gray dawn, conscious of his cramped muscles. He was cold and uncomfortable. He flung out a hand still half in dreams, and his groping fingers touched empty air. Where on earth was he?

Then he realized that he was almost fully dressed; sat up on the edge of the couch where he had spent the remainder of the night, and took his rusty brown head between his hands and remembered.

Dolores had said that their marriage was a mistake. And he had agreed with her.

The mistake was not in the marriage itself, but in getting married at all he thought. In order to have Dolores for his own he had sacrificed his principles, thinking that after all the spirit could be kept, if not the letter. With what high hopes and stammered vows they had sat together in the greening park and dedicated themselves to a marriage that would leave them free. Well, it hadn't. You couldn't beat the game, after all.

He heard Dolores stirring in the bedroom. Presently she came out, very pale, and walked past him to the kitchen. Over a faded linen house frock she had buttoned on an old, disreputable sweater of his.

He went into the tiny bathroom, washed and shaved. When he came out the table was laid, and the coffee pot smoked cheerfully. They sat down and ate in a deathly silence which each hated and neither could break. But after the hurried meal was choked down and Dolores had carried the dishes away he lighted his pipe and sat down, and pretended to read the paper while he waited for her. When she returned—for the apartment was so constructed that, short of locking herself in the bedroom, she could not escape him—he said in a strained, unnatural voice,

"Hadn't we better talk things over quietly?"

She pushed the hair out of her eyes and looked at him wearily. Beauty of contour remained to her but all her glory of coloring and animation was erased. Her magnolia white skin, generally as luminous as pearl, looked dull, her eyes were reddened, set in deep circles, her little nose pink, and her mouth was straight and hard.

"What things?"

She sat down and faced him. He said, terribly embarrassed, feeling her a stranger to him:

"Last night . . . what you said . . . about our marriage being a mistake."

"You said it too," she reminded him.

"Yes. . . ."

There was a heavy pause and then she asked, hopelessly:

"But what can we do about it, Peter?"

To his wrath and amazement he found his mouth shaking. He set his teeth into his underlip, waited until he had controlled his nervousness, and then answered, briefly:

"We can get out of it. . . ."

Her eyes widened, she shrank, twisting her hands.

"Divorce? Oh, Peter . . . no!"

All her ancestors called out to her. Brewster women did not divorce their men.

"I didn't mean that. We can get it annulled," he said.

"Annulled?" She was puzzled, frowned a little. "I don't understand."

"We were under age," he told her shortly. "It can be done . . . easily. If you agree with me, I'll see someone about it to-day. Bill Gaines has a brother who is a lawyer. He can advise us."

She made an odd little gesture, palm up, as if she were letting go of everything to which she had hitherto held.

"All right," she said.

78

He stood up and came closer to her and looked down. "Dolores, I'm awfully sorry," he said.

"It wasn't your fault any more than mine," she told him in a low voice, "I—we just couldn't make a go of it, that's all."

He started to speak, checked himself. She was so forlorn and childish, sitting there. He wanted to take her in his arms. But he couldn't. He felt as young as she, and as helpless. After a moment he cleared his throat and said awkwardly:

"Well, I'll go along now."

He got his hat and overcoat. She did not move until long after the door had closed upon him. She listened to his footsteps going down the outer hall, and wondered if, and when, she would wake up. This was the end, she supposed, dully. It didn't seem possible somehow. She sat there and looked back over her long comradeship with the boy who had just left her. What had become of it? Where were their hopes and their ambitions? What had happened to their love?

Marriage, she told herself, was a trap that sprang, slaughtering everything delicate and lovely and essential. Well, they were through with marriage, she and Peter. He would never forgive her for having "forced" him into it, she supposed.

She wondered vaguely if she had been "brave" that morning in the Park would she be sitting there now listening to footsteps, long departed, but which, she thought, must echo in her heart forever?

She rose and went into the kitchen and began washing up. Big tears dropped into the soapy water and she brushed them away mechanically with the back of her wet, reddened hand.

She and Peter were going to have their marriage annulled. She tried not to think what Cousin Carolyn and Cousin Sarah would say. She tried not to think of anything, but her brain was like a squirrel in a cage. The thoughts spun around and around incoherent and detached.

She couldn't stay here, of course. She'd have to go some-where else.

When Peter came home he looked haggard. He found her sitting almost as he had left her, a wisp of sewing in her lap. He said, without looking at her:

"I saw Gaines. He'll fix it up. He says that there should be very little difficulty."

"We can't stay here together, now," she said boldly.

"I've thought of that. I'll get out."

"No—I'd rather. Then you can do as you please. You could give the flat up at the end of the month. I'll go. . . ."

"Where?"

"Miss Karsten will take me in."

His old, inconsistent anger flamed up:

"You'd go there?"

"Why not? What did you think I'd do?"

"I don't know . . . go home perhaps," he muttered lamely.

"Home!"

She looked at him with blazing eyes.

"They'd never refuse you, Dolores."

"You must be crazy," she said, her voice rising, "to think I could go back . . . and fold my hands . . . and spend my days listening to them say 'I told you so.' I'd die first!"

"I wish you weren't going to that Karsten woman's," he persisted.

"You haven't any right to tell me where to go, and where not to go now," she reminded him.

He nodded, defeated. Then he said, heavily:

"Do as you think best. I'll hurry things all I can. We'll both have to see Gaines, I suppose. Anyway, you'll let me know where you are, so I can keep in touch with you?"

She nodded. Tears were so easy yet they hurt her so.

Suddenly he dropped down on his knees beside her and put his arms about her with a gesture of the most be-wildered appeal.

"Oh, Dolores," he cried out, "what has happened to us?"

She lifted one cold, shaking hand slowly, as if it weighed

80

a great deal, and laid it on the rusty brown hair. She answered:

"I don't know, Peter. . . ."

He said, huskily:

"It was always you. . . . I never loved anyone else."

"I know. . . ."

"We were so happy," he said, "we were going to be so happy. And now . . . this. . . ."

She was silent, touching his hair. She had belonged to him and he to her. Now they were leaving one another. What had done it?

"I want to go," she told him, "now . . . to-night."

She leaned nearer and kissed him, without any passion, without any tenderness. There was nothing but sorrow in the kiss and infinite regret, and the bitter taste of salt upon their lips.

An hour later he sat alone in the apartment. He sat at his desk, his arms folded across it, and his head laid upon his arms, unstirring.

Dolores knocked at Miss Karsten's door. She wondered, standing on the steps, if she would be home. She hadn't thought to telephone. She had just taken her bags and found a taxi and come down.

Asta Karsten lived in an old-fashioned house, over her basement tea-room. She opened the door, tall and angular in a curious blue gown. Behind her there was light, and the sound of people laughing and talking.

"Dolores!"

"I've come . . ." the girl gasped, suddenly afraid, "I . . . would you take me in until I find a place to live?"

Miss Karsten shut the door and stood with her in the dimly lighted hall.

"Infant . . . what is it? Have you left that young man of yours? Quarrelled?"

"We're not going to stay married," Dolores told her in a heartbreaking voice, "I thought . . . if you could take me? I have a little money of my own? I have to go somewhere until things are settled. I could work in the tea-room . . . all day. I'd work so hard."

Asta put her hand on the girl's shoulder and stood a moment, thinking.

"I'll see you through. I've a room and bath on the upper floor, I rented it for my sister who left me last week. I kept it on. You can have that. I'll take you up and get you to bed. Wait a minute."

She stepped back into the apartment and spoke to her guests. Then she came out, picked up one of the bags, and started up the rickety stairs.

"Be careful of that step there. Come along."

Two flights up to the room at the top of the house. A tiny room, hung in gayest chintz, with a homemade dresser and an iron bed painted blue. An alcove bathroom gave off it.

"Here you are. Now get out of your clothes and into that bed . . . luckily it's made up fresh! Try and sleep, Dolores. I may not get rid of those people downstairs until all hours. But we'll talk in the morning."

Presently Dolores was alone. She fell asleep almost instantly as she was completely worn out. But now and then she turned in her dark dreams and put out her hands, and once she said "Peter?"

In the morning she was awakened by Asta's coming in, sitting down on the foot of the bed, and regarding her.

"Here's coffee. Now tell me all you care to."

Dolores pulled the quilt about her shoulders and took the cup. She noticed dully that it was a part of the tea-room service, thick gray pottery, bright with unusual birds. She drank the coffee and lay back against the pillows Asta pounded into shape for her. Asta set the cup on a table and turned, her hands clasped about her knees.

"You are getting a divorce?"

"No . . . an annulment. We were under age. We ran away from home."

"Where is home? Child, I know nothing about you, remember. Have you no people?"

Dolores told her. About the quiet town and the old house, and the elderly cousins; about Peter, living nearby, his father; about the trouble and the burned manuscripts; and the high resolves.

"We didn't mean to marry. We neither of us believed in marriage. We just went away together and came to New York. But I . . . I couldn't go through with it. I don't know why. Perhaps it was the way that clerk at the first hotel looked at me when they wouldn't take us in. So we went somewhere else. And in the morning we sat in the Park and I told Peter that . . . that I couldn't. Then he said we'd be married . . . that it would . . . be the same . . . that we'd leave each other free. So we went to . . . to Port Chester . . . and were married. . . . That's all. It didn't work, Miss Karsten."

"No," said Asta thoughtfully. "I suppose it wouldn't. Well, don't worry. Stay with me. I'll give you work until you find yourself. You can help me a lot."

She rose and stood looking down on Dolores with the strangest expression, half reluctant tenderness, half pity.

"You're . . . how old?"

"Eighteen."

"A baby. Life's all before you. You won't let this break you, Dolores. You'll go on. You had to fail, you know. It was better to realize your failure and make a fresh start. So many people fail and don't know it. . . ."

Later in the day Dolores telephoned Peter. She told him briefly where she was.

"I see. I've talked to Gaines. Will you meet me at his office?"

He gave her the address and named a time. She asked Miss Karsten's permission to go, and went, sitting uneasily in an outer room until Peter came and took her in to the lawyer.

Gaines was a young man, shrewd and hard. He listened to Dolores' stammered sentences, and to Peter's more controlled explanation. He nodded, brusquely:

"Easy as rolling off a log."

"We lied on the license of course," Peter reminded him guiltily. "What will happen?"

"Nothing. It never does."

He gave them instructions and watched them out. His expression was cynical in the extreme. He remarked to his secretary, a pert bobbed young thing, "There go a pair

83

of precious young fools," and settled to more important work.

On the curb Peter and Dolores halted a moment. She said, a little breathlessly:

"I must go back now."

"I'll send the rest of your things. I'll leave the flat when the month is up. One of the other fellows in the office is looking for a place, wants someone to room with him. Perhaps I'll do. You're . . . comfortable where you are?"

"Yes. Miss Karsten has been so kind."

He started to say, sincerely indignant, "Who wouldn't be!" and stopped. He had not been—always—he thought.

After a moment's silence, embarrassing them both, he said, briefly:

"Well, good-by. I'll let you hear from me. . . . Have you . . . money?"

His hand went to his pocket. She cried out, uncaring who heard her:

"I won't take money from you, Peter."

He shrugged, and turned. A moment later they were lost to one another in the crowds, going their separate ways.

CHAPTER XI

"Your case will come up before Judge Eldredge," Gaines told Peter. "He'll want to see you and Mrs. Comstock. That's his procedure in such instances. He's a shark on domestic relations. He never gives up hope of a reconciliation. Be prepared for that."

Dolores and Peter had their first interview with Supreme Court Justice Eldredge one blowing, snowing day when sudden gusts revealed pale, hide-and-seek sunlight, and rifts of blue sky. They were both secretly awed, facing the quiet, elderly man back of his great desk in his chambers.

He fingered the papers on his desk—looked at them over his glasses. Why, these were children, nice children, forlorn and mistaken.

"So you wish an annulment of your marriage. Just why, exactly?"

Peter said, stumblingly:

"We haven't been able to make a go of it."

"You haven't given it a very long trial," the judge reminded him.

Peter flushed, painfully.

"I know that, sir. But I think . . . we think . . ."

"Suppose you begin at the beginning. Never mind how much I know already. Pretend I know nothing. Tell me all you can."

Halting at first, then growing eager with desire to make this friendly stranger understand, Peter told him everything, assisted by an occasional deft question.

"So you didn't believe in marriage? And you still think that if you had not married everything would have gone along smoothly?" asked Judge Eldredge. He did not look skeptical, nor amused, nor shocked. His face was quite expressionless, save for friendliness.

"Yes, sir."

"You think that it was marriage . . . the legal, formal tie which caused you to . . . shall we say . . . haul down your banners? That without the sanction of the law you two young people might have gotten along very well together?"

"Yes. . . ."

Eldredge sighed. He was looking at the girl now, at her vibrant face, her clean, youthful beauty.

"And you agree with your husband, Mrs. Comstock?"

Dolores nodded.

"It has to be so, hasn't it?" she appealed to him directly, "otherwise . . . what happened?"

"Oh, a number of things, perhaps. Circumstance; comparative poverty; the difficulty of adjustment; your youth. You never thought of all that did you? Well think now. Think hard. Would you be willing to try again?"

He looked at Peter but it was Dolores who answered, touching her breast in an unconsciously dramatic gesture:

"I . . . couldn't. . . . Don't ask me to, Judge Eldredge. I couldn't face it again. It was all so different from what I had thought it would be . . . and Peter, too . . . I hamper him, I'm in his way. We promised each other liberty, as complete as if we hadn't married. But we couldn't give it to each other. Don't you see?"

"Perhaps. Yet you still care for each other," Eldredge stated, quietly.

Dolores flushed and dropped her eyes. Then she raised them and met the intense blue of the glance that held hers behind the glasses.

"I've never cared for anyone else," she murmured.

There was a silence. Then Dolores said, suddenly,

"But something's gone—I don't know what it is."

"Romance," Eldredge said, "romance, that couldn't

face life. You've not grown up yet, you know, either of you."

After a moment he put his finger tips together and looked at them wisely and gently.

"What is it you ask, both of you, from life?"

"Freedom!" Peter cried out and Dolores nodded.

"You couldn't find it together? You think you'll find it apart?" he asked and sighed and shook his head when he had looked into their uncomprehending eyes.

"It is my duty, as I see it," he said after a time, "to try and dissuade you from this step. Of course, legally speaking, it's cut and dried enough. But I'd like to give you time to think it over."

"It's no use," Peter told him, sullenly.

"Perhaps not. But it is in my charge now. You will be notified, of course."

He rose, shook hands with them, dismissed them. He said seriously as they were leaving:

"I'm sorry . . . very sorry."

When he was alone he sat quite still and thought. Once he laughed a little, and once the keen eyes were misty. He'd give them time, he thought, delay things, see what came of it. There was no need of haste. There had been far too much haste already.

When they were outside Dolores asked Peter:

"He'll sign the paper?"

"Yes, I suppose so. Gaines tells me he takes his time, does things his own way. There's nothing to do but wait."

They parted and that afternoon he went to see Felicity. She was distrait but glad to see him. Her poet had turned out . . . unpleasantly. An impetuous person, who, whatever his verse, was a rank materialist in his life. He hadn't understood her interest in him. He'd said uncalled for things.

She listened to the reported progress of the comedy, the lack of progress with the peddled drama.

"You mustn't give up hope," she said, blithely, "we will reach our goal yet. Provided," here she stopped and looked at him with slightly narrowed eyes, "provided you don't do anything foolish."

"Such as?" he questioned.

"Well . . . fall in love." She waited and he said nothing. She went on, a little disconcerted, "or . . . get married. That would be the ruin of you, at your age."

Peter took a deep breath. Better confess and have it over. Gaines said that they could keep the matter out of the papers, but one never knew.

"I've . . . been married," he told her steadily, "for a little while. My wife and I are separated."

Felicity looked at him in a mingling of interest, astonishment and annoyance. To think that she never knew! And she'd fancied that she was wholly in his confidence!

"Why didn't you tell me?" she asked, gently reproachful. "I thought we were good enough friends. It hurts me to think that you would keep such an important thing from me."

Peter said, lamely:

"I didn't think you'd be interested."

"Who is your wife?"

"A girl . . . back home. We ran away . . . last spring. We've filed a petition for annulment."

"I see." Instantly Felicity pictured Dolores in her mind, a pretty, small-town girl, sentimental as a greeting-card.

After a moment she added:

"I'm sorry, Peterkin. But I'm glad you found out in time. You mustn't be hampered at the beginning of your career."

"We promised to leave one another free," Peter told her with a wry smile, "but it didn't work."

"No, it rarely does." Felicity sighed understandingly as if she herself were bound at every turn. Van Anden would have been amused had he heard her. "No, artists should never marry. . . ." Her voice trailed off and she looked into the fire, with dreaming blue eyes.

Her interest in Peter was reviving. He had been so simple to read, she thought, a blank book upon which no woman had inscribed her name. But she had been mistaken. He was married all along, leading his own life apart from her influence. That he could have kept so much from her seemed incredible. She was consumed with curiosity about Dolores.

"What is she like?"

"Who?"

"Your wife. . . ."

"She's lovely," he said, slowly, "dark and tall—she looks very Spanish—she's awfully young of course. . . ."

Felicity felt a chill. She pulled up the sable collar of her mauve and blue tea gown. Youth! Youth which was leaving her—the youth she craved and sought vicariously.

"I see," she said, somewhat coldly. Peter did not hear her.

After a minute when she stirred in her great chair he turned and looked at her.

"I've been boring you? And you're angry at me!"

"No, dear Peter."

"You've been heavenly-kind," he told her eagerly. "If it hadn't been for you I would have . . . oh, I don't know what I would have done! Probably I'd have chucked over my job, torn up everything I've written, taken Dolores and gone home. We would have been caught for good then, in the mills . . . and the old house. I've always hated them."

"Mills?"

"My father's."

"You've never told me much about your home," she said.

He laughed.

"There's not much to tell. I was expected to go into the business, of course."

"But you'll have to, one day," said Felicity, thoughtfully.

"As to that, I don't know," he answered, carelessly. "I've no idea. I haven't heard from my father since . . . since we left, except once. He wrote then to offer us board, lodging and a job . . . take it or leave it, he said, in no uncertain terms. So, I left it. I supose when he hears of . . . of the annulment, he'll disinherit me. Not that it matters. . . ."

Oh, youth, again! Felicity looked at him enviously. To be able to feel that it didn't matter.

"You'll not tell him at once?" she asked curiously.

"Lord, no . . . I haven't the nerve. Sooner or later, he'll have to know. Not that I care, as I said, but . . . well, he'll write, and maybe he'll come down to New York and try and show me the error of our ways."

"You'll be lonely now," she told him after a pause, and added as he nodded, setting his lips and frowning a little, "come to me, won't you? I'll try and give more time to the play. Don't keep me from your confidence again? You'll let me be your friend . . . and help you?"

He left her feeling that he wore her invisible favor upon his sleeve.

"Artists should never marry," she had said. But she had married. Perhaps his first instinct had been right and she was not happy with Van Anden. How could she be? They had nothing in common.

He sent Dolores' belongings to her, among them the books he had given her. When she unpacked them she sat upon the dusty floor of her bedroom and regarded them with disgust. Books! What did the books know? She piled them up in a corner, stood over them, and then with a childish impulse pushed them with her foot, angrily, scornfully. They toppled over and settled on the floor again, some of them open, all of them sprawling in a sort of mute reproach.

Contritely, she built them up again. Her hands touched one or two with a reluctant affection. These Peter had marked for her to read . . . a thousand years ago. They were the books upon which he and she were to model their lives, and standards. Well, they had failed, the books and Peter and herself.

The work at the tea-shop wasn't hard and it was amusing. She wrote home, but admitted herself too cowardly to write the truth as yet. She said Peter was very busy, and added that they had moved. And so they had. There was no untruth in that statement.

She met entertaining people. They were gay and friendly and asked no questions. Lucie was curious of course, and had to be told. Dolores had never liked Lucie, but she was grateful to her for having introduced her to Asta Karsten.

With the men she was amazingly shy. Asta teased her. "One would think you'd never known a man except that precious young egotist of yours."

"I haven't, really!" Dolores confessed.

"No?" Asta stared. "Well, it's time you learned your way about. Some of these boys are nice. They'll amuse you. Don't freeze them. We need patronage for the shop and plenty of it."

Shyly, very consciously Dolores tried to be "friendly." She found that the first strangeness soon lessened. These men teased her, made much of her, were impersonally personal to an alarming degree, but she became accustomed to it. They thought her older than she was and were puzzled whether her attitude was a pose or not. They couldn't make up their minds.

One of the most puzzled . . . and the most interested . . . was a man named Boris Ramsay, half Russian, half American. He illustrated for the magazines, and painted portraits. The walls of Peacock Feathers were his doing.

One night, after dinner:

"I'm doing a series of magazine covers," he informed Dolores, staring at her with temperamental black eyes, "The Melting Pot, or something. Girls' heads. Scandinavian-American, Italian-American and so on through the whole list. You're just what I want for the Spanish-American. Would you sit?"

She was thrilled and showed it, but hesitated. Asta, passing at the moment, was drawn into counsel.

"Sit away, Dolores, he's harmless enough. But you must give her the original, Boris, and we'll hang it here. . . ."

"Done!"

So in the mornings, for a time she went to his ramshackle studio around the corner and shivered in a cold room while he sketched her. She had her great grandmother's black mantilla, it had come with her from home, and he provided a rose and a fan.

"You're very beautiful," he told her carelessly as the picture neared an end, "and you don't know it. You will some day. God help us all then! For you have more than beauty . . . you have gallantry, ardor . . . glamour. You'd throw your bonnet over the windmill for a man, I think . . . if you loved him."

As she said nothing, only flushed, he looked up at her sharply.

"You've not loved . . ." he said.

"I've been married," said Dolores uncomfortably.

His face changed, in an instant.

"So? Asta did not tell me." He stepped away from his easel and came toward her, short, slender, treading like a cat.

"Married? Yet I swear you have not loved. . . ."

He flung an arm around her, turned her startled face up to meet his gaze.

"Don't struggle . . . you mustn't be so . . . *prude* . . ." he said, softly, and laughed.

She freed a hand and struck him across the eyes. She was as tall as he and almost as strong. She got to her feet and went to where her wraps lay.

"I'm not coming back again, *ever* . . ." she said, unsteadily, her face white with rage.

"As you wish, my dear."

He made no move to detain her. After all the picture was done. But . . . these chaste, wedded Dianas—amusing they were—how unexpected. He lit a cigarette and mused on her unknown story. Where was the husband? Why, in heaven's name, wasn't he around?

Some men were fools, thought Boris.

CHAPTER XII

"WHAT on earth's the matter?" Asta inquired when Dolores, reaching home, found her alone in the tea-shop, casting up accounts.

Dolores, her eyes dark with rage, told her, sketchily.

Asta laughed.

"He wouldn't have eaten you!" she commented.

"He's a disgusting creature!"

"No. He's rather dear. He didn't try to stop you from leaving the studio, did he? I thought not. Really, Dolores, you are too young to be true."

"He'd been so pleasant," Dolores mourned suddenly, "and then to change . . . like that . . . all in one moment . . . when I told him I'd been married."

"You've a lot to learn," Asta informed her casually, "and you'll learn it hard, I fancy. You've got two ancestries warring in you, you know. One's New England, and the other's Madrid."

Dolores was silent. Then she confessed, slowly:

"I was angry and frightened. I'd never . . . not in all my life . . ."

"You mean?" Asta questioned, an eyebrow raised.

"I mean—men. There never was anyone but Peter, you know."

"I see. Sheltered all the way. And now you're on your own. You'll come through all right. But, have you ever stopped to think how it would have been if you hadn't married Peter . . . if you'd just come away with him?"

Dolores made round eyes.

"But he would have been there, always!" she answered.

"Ah, would he?" mused Asta cynically. "Perhaps. One doesn't know. With the best intentions in the world, my dear, he couldn't have given you much protection. . . ."

Boris strolled into the tea-shop that evening. He leaned over the desk where Asta sat and asked, smiling a little:

"She told you, I suppose?"

"Yes. It was foolish of you. She's very young, Boris. She can't understand your casual ways."

"Lord, I meant her no harm!"

"Don't I know it! Had it been some others I could mention . . . ? However, let that pass. She's learned one lesson anyway. She's very angry with you—a little frightened—and . . . waking up. Make your peace if you can."

"She told me she'd been married!"

"She has been for a matter of months. She's eighteen. She was brought up by elderly cousins in a New England town. She eloped from there with the boy she married. That's her story. Fill in the gaps for yourself."

"It's incredible!" he murmured.

He sat down later at a small table and as Dolores passed him, her head averted, he put out a long hand and touched her arm. She had seen him come in and was furious that he had dared.

"You won't forgive me?"

She shook her head violently.

"At least you'll give me my dinner?" he sighed.

Presently she brought the soup in a little painted bowl and set it down before him.

"Sit here a minute. I want to talk to you—paternally. Oh, don't frown and turn away. Asta won't like it if you make a scene, and I'm very persistent."

Ungraciously she sank into the chair opposite and faced him, her elbows on the table, her chin in her hands.

"That's better. I'm sorry I frightened you away, Miss Muffet. I meant you no ill. You'd come to the studio in good faith, and I had no harmful thoughts. I'm not a hunter of women, my dear. But you're dangerously pretty. You have an unconscious and perilous charm far deeper

94

than your white skin. You'll recognize it some day, and then something of it will be lost, alas! A kiss, a little kindness, what do they matter, after all? Forgive me, be friendly with me if you can."

His voice held the tenderness with which one speaks to a child. But his eyes paid her womanhood full tribute. In spite of her anger and her distaste and her remembered terror, she felt her heart stir faintly. No man had looked at her so—except Peter; and his look had been different—demanding—possessive. A sensation of power came to her . . . and when Boris stretched his hand across the table, she laid her own in it. She'd been foolish, perhaps, looked for actual insult where none had been intended. What an inexperienced idiot he must think her!

"Good!" he smiled. "You needn't come to the studio any more, unless you care to. The picture will finish itself. But you must let me see you—be your father confessor?"

She nodded, after a moment.

"I'm sorry I . . ." She stopped, in a pretty confusion. How absurd it would sound! "I'm sorry I struck you!"

Boris laughed.

"Forget it. Storms clear the air."

"Oh, your dinner!"

She sprang up, relieved, anxious to escape, and hurried to the pantry. Asta looked over at the artist and laughed at the dramatic, exultant wave of his hand toward her.

A night or so later Boris came to Asta's late and found her and Dolores alone, tired out from a busy evening.

"May I come in and borrow your piano?"

"If you don't take it away," Asta said, lazily, from the couch.

He came in, kissed their hands in his exaggerated manner and went to the piano which loomed blackly in the corner. Without another word he sat down in front of it and laid his clever hands on the keys. He drew pictures of pretty girls for a living, but music was his passion.

He touched the keys lovingly, thoughtfully and began to play.

Dolores, lying back in a great chair, closed her eyes. She had never heard such playing. The instrument sobbed,

95

and pleaded, and triumphed, and surrendered under his hands. It was melancholy with all the vast regret of life itself. It laughed through tears. It was a dirge, and a prayer, and a love song. It was both lonely and companioned.

A thin film of ice melted from her heart and something stirred there, perfumed and wistful as her own native Mayflowers. The tears crept from beneath her closed lids. She clenched her hands until she felt the thrust of nails. Peter . . . Peter . . .

She had not known how much she missed him until the music spoke. She had tried not to think of him, save remotely, as someone she had loved, and whom she had put away from her. Now she remembered his eyes in laughter, and his mouth sculptured to a sacred gravity when he bent to lay it upon her lips, her throat. Now she remembered the way his hair grew, and the eager flushing of his face, and the little stammer in his voice when he told her how much he loved her . . . and forever.

She turned, uneasily. Couldn't you tear these memories from your heart and life? Must they remain always?

Boris was playing something very gently now, a cradle song. Suddenly Dolores rose and ran from the room. He turned from the piano in astonishment as the door closed behind her, lifting his hands from an unfinished chord. Asta looked across at him.

"You shouldn't have done that to her. . . ."

"But . . . Heavens, I wasn't thinking of her, poor child! I was restless. I needed the music, that is all. What *have* I done?"

"God knows. I think she stirs in her sleep," Asta told him and a curious look—half tragic, half mystical, but wholly Norse—clouded her clear keen features.

"She has temperament," Boris said, after a pause, "emotion. One sees that. Only the surface has been touched, so far. This marriage of hers . . . I fancy it as half dream, two children playing at love. She has a hard way to go, and a long way. . . . I wonder . . . I wonder . . ."

Asta sat up on the couch, abruptly.

"I intend to take care of her. I've grown fond of her, somehow. Oh, much of it is her beauty. If she were homely,

96

crippled, I'd not care, I suppose. But she came to me like a lovely bewildered child, not knowing where else to turn. I'll look after her. But I wouldn't be doing her a kindness if I kept her wrapped in cotton-wool. She has to learn to face facts, she has to learn to meet life, to beat it to its knees if necessary. I shan't spare her hard knocks. . . . I'll just stand by and see her through." She laughed, shortly. "It's a new role for me. I've made such a mess of my own life so far. I suppose you think it . . . the blind leading the blind?"

"No," he came over to her, grave and concerned, sat down and took her hand, "no—I don't think that. I wish you'd marry me, Asta."

She smiled. It was not the first time he had asked her.

"My dear, I'm five years older than you, and through with marriage. And you don't love me."

"I do. In the way you know. I need you, what's more. Doesn't that count? I'm a fool about women, of course, their loveliness, their helplessness, their pitiful daring. If we married I'd be faithful to you . . . in all that mattered."

"Oh, hush, Boris . . . it's not fair . . . after your music. Listen . . . I had an offer reach me to-day . . . a friend of mine is running a tea and gift shop on a houseboat at Palm Beach. She isn't well, and must give it up. But it is too successful she writes. She cannot bear to have the work go for nothing. She wants me to come down and take charge. Lucie can carry on here, you know. I'd like to go and take Dolores. It would be . . . like opening the gates of a sophisticated fairyland to her. The season isn't as short as it used to be. Many of the house owners stay down until April. Eva suggests that when the season closes definitely I move the boat to Miami. This real estate boom has brought thousands down there. They will stay on, even through the summer. And until the heat got unbearable her plan would be good. What do you think?"

"What am I to think? I'll be lost without you!" he said in authentic dismay.

Asta rose.

"Run home. I'm going up to talk to Dolores. Somehow

97

—a pricking in my thumbs perhaps—somehow I think that we should go."

She laughed at him a little, touched his slim shoulder with her capable hand, and left him. She went up the stairs and knocked at Dolores' door.

"Who is it?"

"Asta. . . ."

"Come in. . . ."

The room was dark. Dolores was curled up on the bed in a scarlet silk kimono, her long hair on the pillows. Asta turned on a light, sat down and surveyed her.

"It's a pity to sacrifice it," she commented, touching the heavy waves of living darkness. "But off it must come. We must be in the fashion. We are going to Palm Beach!"

"What!"

Dolores sat bolt upright and stared at her.

"Yes. Peacock Feathers has done very well. We can afford the venture."

Briefly she told of the plan, Dolores listening wide-eyed.

"You'd like to go?"

"Oh, so much! It would be heaven. Do you know, sometimes at home I used to dream of the hot, still countries, of flowers I'd never seen, and a blue sea, always laughing. I read everything I could about the tropics—huddled on the window seat, with the snow against the pane."

"The fir and the palm," said Asta, laughing. "Well, you'll come then?"

"Clothes?" asked Dolores, practically.

"We'll manage. Smocks, thin things. Lola, next door, is overstocked. If I take a lot of her things down and sell them for her, on little or no commission, she'll fit us out. I've thought of all that. I'll wire Eva in the morning, turn over the place to Lucie, and we'll go."

"But Lucie," murmured Dolores doubtfully, "wouldn't she be the one to go, really? Your niece and all?"

"She'll stay," said Asta briefly. "She has good reasons. . . ."

That point settled, Dolores was like a child confronted with an unexpected invitation to a party.

"How soon can we go? Oh, it will be wonderful . . . to see all the far places I never thought I'd see. . . ."

"Dear, you're not going to Africa. . . ."

"I know. But to get away!"

"Yes, I thought you'd feel that way."

When Asta left her Dolores lay back on her pillow and dreamed with her eyes open. To put miles between herself and Peter. To begin over again. To be in a place which held no memories of him. To feel the sun, a living presence, to see palms and flowers. . . . And then before she came back again the rupture would be final, the papers signed.

She laughed aloud, for excitement. But a moment later turned her face to the pillows and wept, bitterly.

But perhaps she wouldn't be as lonely there. Perhaps the long nights would not seem as full of ghosts and terrors. Perhaps she would stop dreaming herself back in Peter's arms with everything fine, and clear, and glowing between them.

A few days later, when all the arrangements had been made, she wrote Mr. Gaines of her change of plans and gave him her address "in case he needed it." She added, naïvely, "If Peter asks please just tell him I've gone away for a time."

It was snowing the day they left. Boris saw them off. Lucie was there and half a dozen others, pursuing them into the train with last minute protests and envious warnings, prophecies.

The train pulled out. Dolores sat by the window while Asta "settled in" for the run to Washington. She heard the wheels turn to an alternate rhythm. One was happy, a challenge, a drum beat. The other was heavy and bruising. You're going away, sang one; you're leaving Peter mourned the other.

Well, he'd left her, first, she thought.

CHAPTER XIII

PETER had left the apartment and was rooming in a bed-sitting room—and bath—with the youngster with whom he had become most friendly on the *Star*. The drawback to the place appeared to Peter to be that it was far too near 8th Street. But he wasn't likely to meet Dolores accidentally, and it was beyond possibility that he'd meet her purposely. Besides, he wasn't home often.

"Laff" Maynard, his roommate, was a happy-go-lucky person from the Middle West. He had money—but was easily persuaded that if he wanted Peter as a companion they would have to take the sort of place Peter could afford, as he wouldn't let Maynard shoulder the major part of the burden. Laff was "learning the ropes" because his father owned a string of small town papers scattered through the West and the South, and one day Laff would sit in an office and conduct them all. So far his experience had consisted in being advertising manager of his college periodical. Upon graduating, he had informed his indulgent father, seriously, that the way to learn how to run a flock of small town papers was to observe the manner in which an important one was managed. Hence, he thought he would go to New York and be a reporter for a time. Naturally, an allowance would come in handy, meantime, had he his father's blessing?

He was the most casual soul on earth. He was big and broad with a shock of yellow hair, and small, humorous blue eyes. How he held down any job Peter didn't know.

But he appeared to do it through sheer impudence, and he had a flair for news, and a limitless nerve, a way of squirming through police lines and confronting corpses that was little short of astounding. He was tremendously well liked on the *Star*, even the great Mason indulged him, for some occult reason.

His energy was terrifying and boundless. He would prance into their quarters and yank Peter bodily from his desk.

"Oh, for the love of Mike, stop mewing yourself up like that! You've a hundred years before you in which to write the Great American Drama. There's a good party on. Come along—I need you to watch over me."

Nine times out of ten Peter would go.

His associates on the *Star* knew, of course, that Peter was no longer living with his young wife. Further they knew nothing, but the matter was talked over and gossiped about as is the way of newspaper and other offices. Maynard was fully informed and tactfully silent. He had never met Dolores, and being wholly on Peter's side didn't want to. He pictured her as a "small-town-vamp" and thanked his lucky stars that he had escaped any "over the garden gate entanglements." That no less than three girls back home watched for the postman every morning worried him not at all. Love 'em and leave 'em was his nonchalant motto.

Peter had taken him to Felicity's one day as a great favor, and the result was a chill between them, emanating entirely from Peter, for about two and a half days.

"Well?" asked Peter eagerly, when they had left the apartment, "isn't she wonderful?"

Laff snorted largely.

"I suppose so, if you say so."

"But . . . what do you think?" asked Peter, disappointed and beginning to be angry.

"Well, she isn't very young," said Laff thoughtfully, "and it seems to worry her a bit. She certainly has the claws out for promising lads. You'd be surprised how well she understood me after I'd talked to her six minutes. I know, because she told me so. Hokum and whipped cream! Whatta world! Peter, my idealistic Apollo, put not your trust in ageing actresses!"

Peter muttered something disagreeable, but Laff warmed to his task.

"That husband of hers . . . I liked him, strolling in there and looking around, and grinning a little, and strolling out again. Poor devil. *I'd* hate to marry languor and a vanity case. However, she may be useful to you. Fix upon that as the high light in your idealistic friendship."

Peter flushed angrily, the more so because Felicity's potential "usefulness" was never far distant from his mind. He growled:

"You make me sick! What you can see in a lot of shrieking flappers compared to a sensitive artist like Felicity Hawthorne!"

"Oh, gosh!" Laff groaned. "Well, tastes differ, thank God. I like 'em young, shapely, full of pep. Minds interest me very little, souls even less. And I like to do *some* of the talking, my lad."

After a silence during which they stepped out briskly for the long bracing walk downtown, Laff asked solicitously:

"Say, I didn't put my foot in it, or anything, did I? You're not in love with her, are you? I mean . . . you haven't a mother-complex that I don't know anything about, have you?"

"Don't be an ass. Of course, I'm not in love with her. I admire her tremendously, I'm awfully grateful to her, that's all."

Laff grunted. So far he hadn't seen that Peter had much to be grateful for. The drama was reposing in a desk drawer much soiled and battered from its journeying. The comedy was not progressing.

He wondered, a little worried, if Peter were really in love with Miss Hawthorne; if that were why he and his wife had split up?

But Peter was not, very definitely. Nothing about Felicity Hawthorne stirred his senses. She was like a statue on a pedestal, figure of dreams to be bloodlessly adored, a dim goddess to be placated, the glamour of her profession wrapped about her.

He was through with love, he thought angrily. Through with women, who could not rise above the fettering demands of their treacherous and entrapping desires.

But women, it appeared, were not through with Peter.

He met Marise Townsend at one of the parties to which Laff had been bidden. She was a model in a Fifth Avenue gown shop, and lived—he learned— over a florist's in the west forties. She was sitting alone in a corner, sulkily bored, when he and Laff entered the studio. The cigarette neglected between her fingers was no more smoldering than her eyes. But she looked up as Laff and Peter came in, and her expression changed, slightly.

A few minutes later he found himself beside her, cigarettes at his elbow, and a glass in his hand.

"I've heard of you," said Marise.

"From whom?"

"A man named Gaines."

"Old Bill?"

"No, his brother . . . you're different, a little from what I thought you'd be."

"And what did you think?"

"Never mind."

She leaned back, dark and slender in a wisp of henna chiffon. Peter laughed, oddly excited. Something about this strange sulky girl drew him, he didn't know what.

He found himself telling her about his plays, his ambitions. She listened, not seeming very interested, but making him go on whenever he halted for breath or fancied lack of encouragement.

"Go on . . . don't stop. . . ."

"But you weren't interested!"

"In your life story? I hear one like it every day. But I love your voice."

Peter was disconcerted. He had never met anything as frankly predatory before. It troubled him, for all he thought himself so armored.

After a time they danced. She danced beautifully, but disturbingly. She was tall, but not as tall as he. He looked

103

down at a pale oval face and dark eyes momentarily dreaming. Suddenly he stumbled, missed a step, and his heart hurt with its abrupt, warning throb.

"Nothing. . . . I'm sorry I was clumsy. . . ."

"Oh . . . was it just . . . clumsiness?"

Her face was lifted, her red mouth so near he had only to bend his head and kiss it. No one would have minded, few would have noticed. Such things happened at such parties.

He wanted to kiss her. And she knew it. But he did not and presently they sat down again, and she said:

"You're . . . difficult. When will I see you again?"

But he would not allow himself to be drawn definitely. Shortly after he left. Taking Laff aside, he said:

"I'm tired. . . . I've a day ahead of me to-morrow. I'll go on home if you don't mind."

He went, walking through the deserted streets. He knew, had known when he stumbled, dancing, what there was about this strange girl which had appealed to him so dangerously. He didn't give a snap of his fingers for her. She estranged him with her studied frankness. But she had about her a subtle look of Dolores. In the texture of her skin, under the paint, the darkness of the eyes, the blue tones in the black hair, the roundness of the slender body, she was a meretricious Dolores, sophisticated and adult.

He thought he was forgetting, and had put his little, abortive romance behind him, forever. But he had not forgotten. He remembered too often and too easily. He remembered, lately, only the dear things that were far away. Their childhood, their growing into love, and the knowledge of love. Their dreaming, half shy passion in the great hotel at Briarcliff with the birds singing in the silver dawn mist, and the river pale and gleaming far beyond the wide windows. He remembered her as she slept, faintly rosy, her hand flung out toward him. He remembered too much . . . and too little.

When he reached home that night he ached as though he had been beaten. What had come between them, paling the glory and clouding the stars? He did not know. Was it wholly the loss of his freedom that had irked him; was it wholly what he considered her lack of understanding? How much had been his fault; how much hers; and how much the fault of life itself?

What had he done to her? he thought in a sudden panic, sitting in the shadowy room, under a single green shaded light, his work strewn about the typewriter desk. Where was she now? Why hadn't they been able to talk things out, to dig deep down to the fundamental roots of the trouble? The rupture had come, the chasm had opened between them with, it seemed, the suddenness of an earthquake. A quarrel, angry words, and then the blind rush to be free of each other, to cast off their responsibilities.

There was no hope that they would be reconciled. They had made that clear to Judge Eldredge, he thought, as well as to themselves. They couldn't begin again. The mistake lay in the marriage, as he had feared that it would. But now that it was ended, and they had had time to think, apart from one another, couldn't they meet, as friends, talk, find out just what had separated them?

In the morning he made up his mind to find her, to beg her to talk and to listen quietly, without rancor. Sooner or later they must tell their people. He wondered what she had written home. He must find out, their stories must tally.

Marise called him up at the office that day.

"I found out where you are, you see. Why did you leave, so suddenly? You hardly said good night."

"I had to work."

"Ah, that's stupid of you. You're only young once. Will you come to see me this evening? I'll be alone."

"I can't. I'm on a late shift."

"It doesn't matter. I'll give you supper—breakfast—I'm an owl, never go to bed if I can help it."

"I'll see. I can't promise."

Her voice came over the wires, singing, mocking:

"You're afraid?"

He hung up the receiver and sat there thinking while Laff and Bill Gaines hung over him with a ribald jest or two.

105

Afraid? Of course not . . . what a fool she must think him!

But he was afraid. She was so like Dolores, yet so unlike.

He went to see Felicity instead, snatching an hour in the afternoon. She was cool, and she knew nothing of fevers, his heart would be hushed when he talked to her, she would comfort him unconsciously, bringing him gifts solely of the spirit.

But he found that she had nothing to bring him. She was upset over something that had happened during the evening performance of her play. The new ingénue had stolen her thunder . . . taken practically all the cream of the final curtain. She looked older, she talked incessantly of herself. She didn't care who he was when he came, what he said, as long as he formed an audience. He left presently, unstimulated by the over-sweetened cup of tea she gave him, feeling let down and disappointed. .

He wouldn't go to see Marise.

He did not. He stayed home and worked, in his free time. He worked furiously on the comedy. But, it seemed wooden, graceless.

On an impulse he took the manuscript in his hands and going to the fireplace where big coals glowed, he flung it in. He'd begin over. Something different. Oh, he had it in him, they couldn't beat him, he'd show the world yet!

As he watched the paper curl and blacken, as he watched the little hungry red flames, the dissolution, the turning to ashes, his mind went back to that night in the library when his father had pointed to the fireplace and had said "There lies your blasphemy . . . in ashes."

He felt a glow of the old anger, and rebellion. Then it cooled to a measureless despair. It hadn't been blasphemy, of course. It had been the eager voicing of what he had believed, what he still believed, was truth, a truth for which, perhaps, the world was not yet ready. But truth or not, it had been failure, and what now burned in this different and distant room was failure too.

He had believed in himself. He must do so still. And Dolores had believed in him once.

She did so no longer. He made up his mind that he

would go to her and ask her quite humbly . . . why? Ask her wherein he had failed, wherein lay his lack.

After all, of all the people in the world they had been closest to each other; they had known each other best. It was a pity, he mused somberly, that they had to grow up. If only they could have kept things as they had been in their little romantic world, which had spun to the tempo of a spring wind, which had been arched over by a blue sky, which had been instinct with the perfume of opening blossoms.

But they had run away from it, thinking they took it with them. They had run away from bondage and found themselves still bound. They had loved, they had married, it was over.

But he could go to her, couldn't he, and say . . . let us be friends?

A few days later he found, simultaneously, the time and the courage. He walked into the tea-shop, and went to the desk. A thin blonde girl sat there, one knee under her, frowning at some accounts. She looked up as he came in. It was early in the morning, the first luncheon guests had not arrived.

He recognized her as the girl called "Lucie" whom Hodge Meadows had brought to the house.

"I'm Peter Comstock," he said.

"Yes, I remember."

She regarded him thoughtfully. Why was he here? She owed nothing to Dolores, was jealous of her perhaps. But she was wary by nature, and very close mouthed.

"I wanted to speak to . . . to Dolores," he said, finding, to his annoyance, that he flushed and stammered under her indifferent stare.

"She's South. She and my aunt left a few days ago . . . for Florida."

"Florida!" His jaw dropped comically. "But she didn't let me know. . . . I hadn't heard . . ." he floundered.

Lucie smiled slightly.

"I believe she informed her lawyer," she said delicately malicious.

After that there was nothing he could say or ask. He thanked the girl and walked out.

Florida!

Dull anger woke within him. Not that he cared where she went, or what she did! But she might have told him. After all he was still her husband. No word had reached him that the papers necessary to seal their legal separation had been signed.

He stood on the curb, kicked at it like a sullen small boy, stubbing his toes against the stone.

Florida! She could go off then, for a good time, and he could stay at home and slave himself sick. He hated his work, he hated New York, he hated everything.

As he stood there irresolute, wondering if he should go to Gaines and demand to know what he knew of this inexplicable flight, he remembered that once he and Dolores had planned to go South . . . someday . . . when their ship came in . . . together. . . .

Well, their ship had come in . . . upon the rocks.

CHAPTER XIV

THE houseboat, which was called *The Gilded Sailfish*, for no very particular reason, lay moored to the end of a dock which jutted out in front of a row of pink stucco buildings, which housed shops, a motion picture theater and apartments. *The Sailfish* was extraordinary, square and massive, unexpectedly large. It was painted an impossible jade green, with lines of gold here and there, and under the deck awnings were tables for tea. Below, an unusually large room contained more tables, and a bewildering display of "gifts," everything from Lola's smocks to lingerie and pottery.

The owners of the boat, Eva and Herbert Manton, were itinerant artists, who had turned their marine cottage into a shop when there seemed little sale for Bert's black and white sketches, and Eva's tiny, glowing oils of Floridian landscapes. This was their third season at Palm Beach and they had done very well. But Eva was ill, and Herbert restless, and they were relieved when Asta Karsten, whom they had known for years, accepted Eva's offer to come down and run the shop for as long as pleased her and suited them. Dolores, in a maze of excitement from her first long train journey, and her initial glimpse of palm trees, liked the Mantons on sight, lean, lanky, badly dressed Bert, and his fragile, nervous little wife. She was enchanted by the boat, it was like a toyland, and Bert, watching her move about the "living room" exclaiming over the carved cocoanut baskets which hung from the ceiling, looked at Asta with a slow twinkle in his tired brown eyes.

"You'll have an increase of customers. . . ."

Asta smiled, and said nothing. Bert went on, his teeth showing white in a face tanned to the color of leather:

"The secret of success down here is bigger and higher prices. You'll soon learn. They like to pay through the nose. Did Eva tell you about the dance arrangements we've made this season for two afternoons a week? The boys are stranded college kids, we don't have to pay them much, but we feed them. For the other days there are records and the phonograph on deck. But remember the cover charge when the Ukele Trio are working here."

"Cover charge!"

"Well, why not? It's a skin game, my child, make up your mind to it in the beginning."

The Mantons had already removed their scanty baggage to a small hotel across the bridge in West Palm, and were ready to turn the boat over to the newcomers. There were two tiny bedrooms . . . with "real windows and curtains!" as Dolores exclaimed upon her first sight of them, a miniature bath, and a "galley" that was, except for an absence of tiling, for all the world like a New York kitchenette. But it was compact and practical enough, and the Mantons' colored cook found it adequate for her needs, as no meal save tea was served aboard *The Gilded Sailfish*.

"Luncheon and dinner wouldn't pay," Eva explained, "but if anyone wants to give a private supper and dance aboard, we arrange it with them."

"Liquor?" asked Asta briefly.

"We don't supply it," Bert answered, "they bring their own and we give them ginger ale, or mineral water, or orange juice—at a price."

The Mantons stayed in West Palm for a day or two, to see their substitutes well started, and then left, and before a week had passed Dolores felt that she had been in Florida forever, serving pretty girls in marvellous frocks, and good looking boys in flannels with tea—and—mineral water.

Some one was almost always on the boat, women wheeling by in the morning would stop to buy something they

110

didn't need, the afternoons were always busy, the dance afternoons brought more customers than they could take care of, and already in the first week two evening parties had been "thrown" . . . and thrown far and wide.

"They're asking me to dance," panted Dolores, going below to find Asta, who was busy helping in the kitchen.

"Dance then."

"But . . . but . . . I don't know any of them."

"What does it matter? We're here to make a success, aren't we? Dance then, and drum up trade."

"But my clothes!"

"Run along and don't annoy me."

Well, clothes didn't matter, after all. One or two of the girls wore sport frocks, the rest were in evening gowns except for one young thing, slender and vivid as a flame, who, during the course of the evening, calmly removed the belted linen dress she wore, kicked off her shoes, pulled off her stockings and stood revealed in a scant scarlet bathing suit.

Dolores gasped, watching her as she perched momentarily on the rail, and dived neatly overboard into the quiet, moonlit gleaming waters of Lake Worth.

"But won't she . . . ?" she asked, bewildered, aloud.

"Catch cold?" said a quiet voice by her side as she stood watching, a little apart from the others, "no. She's been leading the simple life all day . . . picnic on the beach since noon. This is more or less in the nature of a wind-up . . . it's Amabel Yates, you know."

Dolores did know. Amabel Yates, twice married, twenty-three, Boston, polo, amateur swimming champion, the girl who wore evening clothes to races, and riding boots to dances if it so pleased her.

She turned to look at the man who had spoken. He was tall and very slender. Immaculate flannels and a double-breasted blue coat, smooth blond hair under the glow of the Chinese lanterns, quiet, wary blue eyes, a clipped fair mustache at which his lean brown fingers were pulling, idly.

"My name's Sterling . . . Kay Sterling," he told her

111

abruptly, in his smooth, easy voice, with the accent she had been taught to call "English." "And yours?"

She told him. He asked casually:

"Miss or Mrs.. . . . ? Not that it matters. . . ."

"M-Mrs. . . ." stammered Dolores, terribly embarrassed.

"What's happened to the Mantons? I've been off fishing."

Dolores told him.

"I see. And you'll be here all season. . . . Do you have any free time?"

Dolores hesitated.

"Well, we'll see. Come on and dance with me."

She gave herself into his experienced arms, a little reluctantly. She felt ill at ease, out of place in this crowd of laughing, careless people. Amabel Yates had climbed back on deck and stood there dripping and smiling dimly as someone dried the uncovered portion of her slim body with a large handkerchief.

Under the lights as they danced Dolores saw that Sterling was older than she had thought him. He had looked thirty in the softer light, now he seemed nearer forty. His face was lined, his mouth a little hard, his eyes were old. But as she looked at him he smiled and his smile made him twenty.

"Like what you see?" he asked her.

She had never grown used to this casual give and take. She flushed a little, and then, boldly resolved on the truth:

"I don't know. . . ."

"That's interesting. Well, I'll give you ample opportunity to make up your mind. . . . Where's your husband?"

"New York," said Dolores abruptly.

"But you're never a New Yorker," he told her, as he guided her expertly and easily over the deck. "Never. Boston is nearer. Am I right?"

Dolores nodded. A little breeze blew in from the Lake and the Palm fronds along the Lake Trail rattled softly together. The stars were very bright and very near, the music had a sweet, melancholy madness, and the moon was a scented flower, so close one could reach up a hand and pluck it from the dark velvet sky.

Suddenly Sterling swung her to a wide-cushioned seat that ran across the stern.

"Sit here a moment. Tell me the story of your life. Not a very long story, I think."

She said, uneasily,

"Someone will want something. Miss Karsten can't attend to them alone."

"Nonsense. They've eaten more than is good for them, and more than they wanted. Besides, I'm host."

Dolores looked at him as he lounged against the cushions, a lighted match in his cupped hands.

"But I thought that Mrs. Redding . . ." she began, wondering, remembering the vivacious little Californian widow who had "ordered" the party and who sat not far away from them now, surrounded by men.

"It's the same thing," said Sterling coolly, and turned to look into her ignorant startled eyes. What he saw there made him smile a little. He went on, not giving her time to speak—or think—

"Tell me about yourself."

"There's nothing to tell."

"We'll see. I'm going to be here—a long time. I've just made up my mind."

He laughed at her over the glowing end of his cigarette. Lazy admiration spoke from every feature of his good looking, rather worn face. Dolores felt her heart beat faster.

"Kay!"

Mrs. Redding leaned toward them from her table and her clear voice held a petulant note. She displayed an empty glass. She was a pretty woman, red-headed, her gown cut too low.

She called him twice before he answered, and Dolores was in an agony of embarrassment. Amabel Yates, a man's coat wrapped around her, laughed maliciously.

Sterling rose and stood looking down at Dolores.

"I'll come aboard in the morning," he said, "and take you for a wheel-chair ride. I want to see if you are as lovely by daylight. So few women are."

He turned and left her. She watched him lean over Mrs.

Redding and take a flat silver flask from his pocket. She could see quite plainly the anger in the woman's eyes, she saw her put her hand on his sleeve and keep it there, possessively.

Some one called her across the deck. Dolores went over, glad to escape from the other group.

It was three o'clock before the last of them left. Dolores and Asta stood by the railing and watched them. Sterling, his arm through that of Mrs. Redding, nodded absently, and passed out of sight, down the deck, and up the trail where yawning chairboys waited. Asta sighed, wearily.

"Well! But it was worth it. They paid a stiff price for an evening's entertainment . . . if you want to call it that. Come to bed, we'll clean up in the morning. I'm half dead."

"Who is that Mrs. Redding?" asked Dolores abruptly when they went below.

"I don't know. I've heard people talking, of course, even in the short time we've been here. California. Living at the Poinciana. No visible means of support."

They slept, rose early and made the boat presentable for the day with the help of amiable Alma, and some recruited cleaning women. And at eleven Kay Sterling lounged across the dock and went below to find Dolores arranging a display of some of the Mantons' work on a table, setting up the small easels which held the sketches and oils.

"Are you ready?" he asked, without further greeting.

She looked down at the smock she wore.

"I . . . hadn't asked."

Asta came in from the bedroom and looked at her early guest coolly. He smiled at her, engagingly.

"Could Mrs. Comstock come for a wheel chair ride? She tells me she hasn't seen anything of . . . the sights," he announced.

"Run along," Asta said amiably to Dolores, "I can take care of anyone who comes in this morning."

But her eyes questioned. Sterling named himself, smiling, and when Dolores ran back for a broad brimmed hat and a dash of powder he said, easily:

"Surely you're not going to let her miss all the good times?"

Asta shook her head, unsmiling.

"No. . . ."

When they had gone she leaned on the rail and watched them up the dock. Her eyes were grave. Presently she shrugged her shoulders and went below again.

Sterling had a wheel chair waiting. He settled Dolores, climbed in beside her, his stick braced between his knees, his blond head hatless, the color of honey.

"Every one's on the links, presently they'll all be bathing," he announced, "we'll have the trails to ourselves."

"But . . . I'm keeping you away . . . ?"

"No . . . one gets tired of the routine."

He whistled suddenly and a huge police dog, more than half wolf, appeared from nowhere and loped steadily beside the smooth progress of the chair.

"My chaperon," he explained soberly, "speaks only German. His name is Fürst."

He turned, as they took the trail which led away from the Lake and up to the ocean, and surveyed her a moment in silence.

"Why . . ." he said softly, "you're only a baby . . .!"

Dolores flushed and Sterling exclaimed,

"Do that again. I didn't know any one could, nowadays."

She turned aside, preserved a chilling silence. Sterling laughed.

"Don't be angry. We'll go to Bradley's for lunch, if it would amuse you."

"I can't!" said Dolores flatly.

"Why not?"

"In a smock!"

"In a shift as far as that goes. Oh, I'm sorry! I don't mean to offend you. It's just the usual currency of speech. If you like we'll stop back at *The Sailfish* and you can change . . . and explain to Miss . . . what's her name?"

"Karsten."

"Quite so. Not that it matters. Tell me why you're here

115

and who you are. Tell me about your husband . . . he must be a madman."

"I . . . Mr. Comstock and I are separated," she said, trying to speak coolly.

"I see. My original opinion holds. A madman . . . worse, a fool."

"Please. . . ."

"All right. We'll defer the argument until later. That house we are passing . . . if we must talk of cabbages and kings . . . that Moorish affair with Belasco trimmings, belongs to the Mullins . . . the razor people. This one, to the Countess . . . well it doesn't matter, she was born Smith and her people make flour. Does local history interest you?"

"Not much," said Dolores honestly. She was beginning to like him even if he made her uncomfortable. "Do you live at one of the hotels?"

"God forbid. I have a house, not far from *The Sailfish*. I'll show it to you one day. It has a history. It was built for a man who carelessly got himself murdered before he could live in it. I bought it if not for a song, at least for an aria. Someday, I'll show it to you, if you care to see it."

"You . . . live in New York?" she asked.

"Is it fair that I should answer all your questions and you should brush mine aside? Yes, part of the time. I've a place in North Carolina, and something they call a Villa in Italy. Now the next thing you must ask me is . . . are you married?"

It had burned on her tongue. She flushed again to remember it. She shook her head, silently, and he laughed and went on:

"Confess. The answer is no. I have been, for ten interminable years. I am no longer. I'll never be again. Freedom," he said, smiling, "freedom is the only thing worth having . . . and the hardest to acquire."

Dolores drew a long breath. Freedom! This careless man beside her, surely he was free? No ties, money, the world before him. . . .

"I think," said Sterling softly, "that you agree with me." She nodded, gravely, one hand linked in the other.

116

"Yes. . . ."

"Good. I'd be interested to know how you came to that conclusion at your age. What is it, by the way?"

"Eighteen. . . ."

"Really? Last night . . . I would have said . . . twenty-two . . . but to-day . . . I'm inclined to believe you. . . ."

He looked at her, long, deeply, yet with no effect of staring. The white, unblemished skin, luminous as pearl, the soft mouth, red as poinsettia, the dark, dreaming eyes that had as yet, he thought, seen very little of life. Eighteen . . . and clamoring for freedom. His heart raced a little. He said to himself, in pleasurable surprise . . . "steady on. . . ."

The chair ran on smoothly, the coal black gentleman on the bicycle behind them singing to himself in a melancholy crooning, but grinning widely. Mr. Sterling was a prodigious employer!

The palm trees sang together, the sun was golden, the sky an untarnished blue. Dolores lay back, sighing unconsciously. She had never felt so . . . relaxed, so warmed through and through, so carelessly happy.

"We'll go back now," Sterling said, after a long silence, "and I'll wait while you change."

"Mr. Sterling . . . ?"

She sat upright, embarrassed.

"Yes . . . ?"

"I haven't . . . I mean . . . the clothes women wear here . . ." she was stammering softly.

"It doesn't matter. Eighteen! They'd give you the gowns off their backs for your skin, my dear," he said lightly, and she felt no affront.

After a pause he added, gently:

"Or . . . if it really matters . . . it could be rectified so easily."

He glanced at her quickly. She had not heard, or if she had, she had not understood.

The chair rolled on in a complete silence, broken only by the soft singing of the happy-go-lucky negro, and the panting of the great dog loping along beside them, sinister and faithful as a shadow.

CHAPTER XV

"I'M giving," said Kay Sterling, a few days later, "a little dinner—the Everglades, I think. I want you and Miss Karsten to come."

He was sitting alone at a table on the deck of *The Gilded Sailfish*. Blue dusk was falling over the Lake and Asta moved about the deck with her quick, free step, lighting the candles in the monstrous blossoms of the Chinese lanterns. Mrs. Redding was sitting with half a dozen people. She looked over at Sterling continuously, and laughed more often and shrilly than the not very humorous comments of her companions appeared to warrant.

Dolores, standing beside Sterling, her tray in her hands, hesitated.

"I don't know," she said, doubtfully, "I'll ask her. . . ."

"I'll ask her myself! Miss Karsten!"

Asta came over to them and stood by Dolores, her hand on the girl's shoulder.

"Mr. Sterling?" she answered, smiling.

"I want to have a dinner party," he explained, "just four of us. You and Mrs. Comstock, and another man. Are you booked for, say, Wednesday?"

Asta looked quickly at Dolores. The girl's face showed nothing but pleasure in anticipation. She nodded, rather brusquely.

"Very well—if it can be late—we're so busy now, afternoons."

He set the time, laid a bill upon his check, and rose,

nodding almost casually to his hostesses. Then he walked over to the other table and pulling up a chair by Mrs. Redding sat down. But not before his quick ears had caught a snatch of conversation between Dolores and Asta.

"I've nothing to wear. . . ."

Asta said, idly:

"The silver?"

"So old now—it's tarnished. I saw a frock in Berthe's window—but I couldn't, of course."

Mrs. Redding had turned a sulky shoulder upon Sterling. He touched her arm, now smiling.

"Angry at me?"

"One never sees you any more," she said, low.

"Ah, I'm a bird of passage," he answered, pleasantly, "and more apt to linger where no cages are provided."

"I haven't tried," she began, eagerly, while the other people at the table pretended not to listen and strained their well-bred ears in the process, "you know I haven't. . . ."

A little later the party, the last on the boat, left and Sterling with them. Asta and Dolores were below, he made no attempt to speak with them again. He would see Dolores in the morning, she was going for an early swim with him.

Over their supper Asta said suddenly to her companion:

"I determined when we came down here that you were to have a good time. Dancing, people, laughter, all that sort of thing. I wasn't going to warn you . . . about anything. You've not had a very gay youth, I wanted you to have it, in reason. As to warning . . . I have no right to interfere, anyway, and besides, as I told you, admonitions are against my principles. But Sterling is interested in you. This isn't another case of . . . Boris, for instance. Sterling, from all I hear, isn't . . . eligible . . . if you're thinking of that."

Dolores flushed, indignantly.

"I . . . I had no such idea," she said in the soft stammer that afflicted her when she was embarrassed. "He's been very nice, that's all. What did you mean by . . . eligible?"

"I mean, he isn't a marrying man . . . not again. . . ."

119

Dolores flung up her round chin and her eyes burned.

"As if I cared! I'd not marry again! You know that, Asta!"

"Yes. That is, I've heard you say so before. Well, that's all I wanted to say. Sterling is experienced and charming. The odds are all against you if you think to play his game, that's all. By the way, have you heard anything from New York?"

"No. Just Mr. Gaines. He wrote that things were delayed, he didn't seem to know why."

"I see. And from home?"

The round chin was lowered and the white lids fell:

"Cousin Carolyn writes. . . . I've been to afraid to tell her . . . anything. I said . . . I had an opportunity to come down for the season with a friend . . . and she was scandalized . . . !"

"I suppose so."

"She said in her day it was a woman's duty to remain with her husband."

"So it was," said Asta, laughing, as Alma came in to clear away. "Dolores, you can't put off telling them forever."

"No. . . ."

A little later Asta heard her wail softly from the bedroom. She went in and found her contemplating the shabbiness of the silver frock.

"I've worn it so little,' she complained.

Asta said, soothingly:

"Perhaps you'll find something. The season isn't young, there will be sales. Go to Berthe's again to-morrow."

Dolores heard her, vaguely. She was still fingering the tarnished silver dress, thinking back . . . the dress she had worn the night of their quarrel.

She rose and put it away, tenderly, as one banishes a ghost.

She could afford a new dress, she thought, lying awake that night, listening to the music that came to her faintly from some house on the Trail. Asta paid her, liberally. There were tips which as yet she was not quite accustomed to taking for granted. And she had her little income. But it would have to be a simple dress at a far simpler price than she had yet seen at Palm Beach.

In the morning she was ready when Sterling called for her. They rode down to the beach under a sky that was blue pearl. The day was warm, almost windless and the ocean, as blue as if the sky had fallen, lay almost without motion under the hot sunlight.

Dolores swam well. She could not remember the time when she did not swim. Her slender, round body in the green suit, her dark hair, which she had had cut before she left New York, perking out in two flat whirls from under the tight green cap, the lovely tones of her skin unblemished in the pitiless light. Sterling looked at her and sighed audibly. She was the loveliest thing he had seen in years, unflawed, unspoiled. Of course, he mused, idly, one would tire of that naïve dewiness, that utter lack of sophistication. But before one tired it would be piquant.

"Do you know how pretty you are?"

"Please don't say things like that. . . ."

He lounged beside her on the sand, tanned, and lazy, one hand caressing his mustache, hiding his mouth.

"You are delicious when you stammer . . . such a child."

She said hurriedly:

"It's been lovely . . . but I must get back."

"Why? It's a long way to tea time."

"I know. . . . I wanted to shop . . . the one right by the boat. . . ."

"Berthe's?"

She nodded.

"What shall you do there?"

"Look at clothes," said Dolores laughing, "and wish I could buy them. Then come away again."

He said, idly:

"There were lovely things in the window. . . . I stopped to admire them last evening when I left you. The women I was with have never been known to pass a shop without pausing . . . hopefully."

Dolores asked, like a little girl:

"Did you see the one with the metal cloth bodice and the lace skirt?"

He nodded, and asked:

"You like it?"

"It is adorable," she said, sighing.

"Buy it then," he suggested, "it was never designed to languish in a window."

"I priced it," she told him solemnly, "and it was far too much."

"That's a pity," he told her, laughing, "price it again. Saleswomen are open to reason, very often."

After he had dressed he went to a telephone and had a little conversation with a certain lady who managed to be fat and serpentine at the same time, like a boa constrictor after a full meal. Then he came out and waited, smiling, for Dolores.

He left her at the dock and leaned from the chair.

"You haven't looked at your dress!" he accused her.

She glanced back at the pink shop, directly in front of the dock.

"Oh . . . what's the use?"

"Why not?" he asked and smiling, signed to the chair boy and the dog, and went on.

Dolores hesitated. Then she turned and went back to the shop which said sedately *Berthe . . . Gowns* across the window in gilt. Perhaps there would be something left over from one of the early consignments.

When she went in Berthe herself, plump and sinuous in a black and white sport frock, rose to greet her.

"Mademoiselle wishes?" asked Berthe with a delightful accent. Presumably there had been a French quarter in her native Brooklyn.

"I wondered . . ." hesitated Dolores, "an evening frock . . . not very expensive?"

Berthe pulled a gilt chair forward for her prospective customer and looked toward the two unoccupied saleswomen who were whispering in a corner. One of them sprang to attention.

"Show Mademoiselle the painted chiffons," demanded Berthe.

They brought, and displayed, gowns like woven flowers. The price tags were inconspicuous but—once seen—never forgotten. After half an hour of delight and despair Dolores said hopelessly:

"They're lovely. . . . I'm sorry, but they are too expensive, Madame Berthe."

Berthe uttered an exclamation in what might have been a Latin language. She asked, as if she had just remembered,

"Now I recognize Mademoiselle. From the house boat, is she not?"

"Yes. . . ."

"After all," concluded Berthe musingly, "we are, in a way—how do you say it?—professional comrades. I have a gown or two laid aside . . . very much marked down. But ruinously! For special customers, for my friends, you understand. Wait, one little moment, I beg you."

She whispered an order to the blonder saleswoman, who, preserving an impassive countenance, presently came forward with three frocks draped carelessly over one arm. Dolores gasped. One was the darling in the window. She pointed it out, almost speechless with excitement.

"That one!"

Berthe smiled, graciously.

"A French model. It would become Mademoiselle to perfection."

She took it from the saleswoman and nodded a dismissal. The blonde retired, smiling faintly. A very important customer, if Berthe bothered her indolent self . . . and yet she wore a linen gown that had probably cost twelve-ninety-five in a department store!

Berthe stood up, shook out the lace of the skirt and held it up to her own astonishing figure.

"Mademoiselle will try it on?"

Dolores rose, lost. She could never afford it . . . but . . . she would not resist the temptation to feel it once, clasping her, falling about her, lovely and gleaming. She followed Berthe into a dressing room.

The dress was charming. The tight plain bodice was of metallic cloth, silver, green and peacock blue with curious rosy lights, the skirt, short and full over a wired petticoat was of Spanish lace, dead black, and on the shoulder, one half-opened flower.

Dolores slipped into the frock and stood there a moment before the mirror. Her hair, which had been cut very short in back, but which waved slightly from her forehead, reflected the metallic gleams. Her skin was whiter than blossoms, and her mouth a scarlet fruit.

"It is lovely," said Berthe sincerely, "it will bring me more customers . . . if you wear it."

Dolores still looked at herself in the mirror. She asked just above a whisper . . .

"How . . . m-much?"

Berthe named a price, less than a third of that which was marked on the price tag.

The hot color shot up in Dolores' face.

"Oh . . . but!" she began, incredulous, while Berthe, mindful of her instructions, repeated firmly:

"Reduced . . . because of the season. But I had saved it . . . for special reasons . . . to sell to a friend, perhaps."

Dolores looked alarmed.

"But you'd let me have it?"

"Certainly," agreed Berthe amiably, helping her to take it off. "Shall I send it to the house boat? It needs no alteration."

Later, Dolores displayed the gown to Asta and named the price.

"Isn't that marvellous?"

"It is," agreed Asta, puzzled, "I don't understand . . . however the woman is probably overstocked."

So on the night of Sterling's dinner Dolores wore the Berthe gown. She was as conscious of it as a child of her first party dress. Asta watched her smiling, as she danced with their host. The other man, an older man, rather attractive and with odd sleepy eyes commented casually:

"Kay's badly smitten. . . . I don't blame him. . . . Is that girl Spanish?"

"She has Spanish blood . . . but far back," Asta answered looking about the beautiful crowded room.

"I thought so—but would have sworn it was in a very near generation. She is lovely."

"So you bought your dress?" Sterling was saying.

"Yes . . . it had been reduced . . . do you like it?"

"Very much. It's worth any price you paid for it," he told her gravely. "Every one is looking at you . . . the men as if they could eat you, the women as if they could kill you."

She laughed.

"Don't be silly!"

He took her home, Asta following with the other man. In the wheel chair, wheeling up the Trail, he suddenly took her hand in his.

"Dolores . . . you like me a little?"

She gasped, trying to pull her hand away.

"Please . . . yes, very much," she said honestly.

"Not more than that."

"Mr. Sterling. . . ."

He freed the hand, leaned back, lighted a cigarette.

"Well, it's enough to go on . . ." he told her, quietly.

She was trembling a little, from embarrassment, from fright, from excitement. His hand had been cool and hard and . . . holding. She had felt its strength.

When he had left her she went aboard the boat and waited for Asta. She sat down surrounded by the careful litter of things, the potteries and smocks and bits of hammered silver jewelry, and twisted her hands in her lap. She felt alone and frightened. Her heart beat terribly. No man had ever stirred her save Peter. But this man . . . might. She tried in vain to think coherently. She only knew that she liked him and that he troubled her. She had wanted to . . . leave her hand where it had been, warm in his own. She had wanted to . . . yet she didn't love him! She'd never love anyone again! Loving hurt too much! Was it possible she thought, amazed and reluctant, that you could be emotionally disturbed by a man you didn't love, by something in his light touch and glance, and in the tones of his voice, something that made your soul purr like a contented cat?

That night Dolores woke from dreams in which she had been in Peter's arms. Then Peter was no longer Peter, but a smiling, casual young man with hair the color of honey and tanned, controlled face. She had fought him, trying to find Peter again.

"Peter . . ." she called.

She woke to find a drenched pillow and Asta bending over her.

"Wake up . . . you've had a nightmare. . . ."

Dolores sat up in bed pushing the tumbled hair from her wet eyes. . . .

"It was Peter," she stammered, still so far from waking that she did not know what she said.

"Lie down," said Asta gently, "and go to sleep. . . ."

"He's not here then?" asked Dolores wonderingly, and even as she asked, lay back, docile as a child . . . and slept again, without dreams, and Asta left her, tall in her vivid kimono, her blue eyes whimsical.

CHAPTER XVI

PETER was restless. The front page seemed further away than ever. He could not write. The comedy lay in a drawer scribbled over, scissored, pasted unevenly together. He said to Laff Maynard, gloomily:

"How can you keep on—keeping on? Parties and all. I'm getting fed up. This town's on my nerves."

"Why? It's a gorgeous hamlet!"

"Full of promise that never comes off," grouched Peter, "nothing ever turns out the way you expect it to. Wish I had the nerve to cut loose and get away—somewhere, anywhere."

"See Marise lately?"

"No," said Peter shortly.

Laff grinned. He was sitting in a shabby Morris chair, his long legs stretched out before him. From a capacious pocket he produced a severely typewritten letter and perused it, groaning gently.

"What's the matter?" asked Peter, stirred out of his dismal preoccupation.

"My old man. Wants to know when I'm really going to work. For gossakes! Tells me there are jobs open on his dinky little papers. Says I'd learn more about the business in a one horse town than in Glorious Gotham. Fears I have too many distractions." He shook the letter and groaned again. "No check enclosed! I wrote humbly, requesting a slight dividend. Man cannot live by wage and on allowance alone."

Peter said, suddenly:

"Wish I had your chance."

"What? General office boy on a jerk water village newspaper? Lad, you're welcome. If you want to change your job I'll find you another. Trust your Uncle Dudley."

"Maybe I'll take you up, some day," answered Peter, not meaning it, much.

He went to see Felicity soon after. She was, as usual, not alone. He sat in a corner and saw her shedding her pale gracious light upon half a dozen eager young men. He felt, watching, curiously adult.

Latterly, she had not given him as much of her time. He had come to a place in his dogged playwriting where he needed more than pretty suggestions and mild enthusiasm. He needed real help. And was determined to get it. Obstinately, he outstayed the others, hoping she would ask him to supper, as it was a Sunday evening.

She did so. Presently they faced one another across the table, the polished wood of which gleamed softly through the meshes of lace, with the candles casting their flickering, favorable light over the cared-for loveliness of her face. She listened as Peter talked of himself, half bored, half tolerant.

One of the Japanese servants came in and told her that some one was waiting to see her. She said, indifferently, "Tell them to wait," and went on playing with an aspic salad. To Peter she said, briefly:

"Jack Garrison . . . you know him, don't you?"

Peter nodded. Garrison was a Southern boy, recently arrived in town with credentials and a trunk full of manuscripts. Felicity added, thoughtfully:

"He's brought someone with him . . . a girl, very talented, they tell me."

Peter said devoutly:

"You're awfully good, you know . . . giving so much of your time to us—aspirants."

She smiled, flashing into momentary interest. As she started to reply, the Japanese reappeared, his usually masked face wrenched into a semblance of humanity. He

128

bent over, whispered something in his sibilant way. Peter saw her go pale under the delicate mask of rouge.

"Miss . . . Ainsworth? I don't understand . . . tell her to come in."

As the man slipped from the room she explained, pushing her plate aside:

"It's . . . Van's office-nurse. . . ."

Before Peter could answer the woman was in the room, terribly disturbed under her obvious control. She stood close beside Felicity and brushed aside her interrogative greeting.

"It's the doctor, Mrs. Van Anden," she said, and Peter thought, wonderingly, that it was the first time he had ever heard Felicity so addressed. "He's had an accident."

There was something angry, or deliberately hostile in the look she bent upon the younger woman under straight graying brows. Felicity murmured, ghastly:

"Accident . . . Van?"

"He sent for me," said Miss Ainsworth. "He asked me to come down and tell you. He doesn't want you frightened."

Peter thought, furiously, . . . he's chosen an odd messenger then! But the nurse was continuing:

"An emergency operation. The knife . . . no one knows how it happened . . . his glove was cut through."

Felicity got to her feet. She was extraordinarily quiet. "Where is he?"

"At the hospital."

"We'll go at once," said Felicity.

She walked from the room without glancing at Peter. He followed, not knowing what else to do. When he moved to her side in the hall he found her maid there with wraps, and a murmured suggestion.

Felicity looked down at the teagown she wore.

"It doesn't matter. Give me that fur cape."

As she stood a moment in the hall while the Japanese ran out, young Garrison came out of the drawing room, eager, expectant.

"Miss Hawthorne? . . . Oh," he explained, his face falling, "you're going out?"

129

Felicity looked at him without seeing him. A dark, attractive girl had appeared behind him, and was looking curiously over his shoulder.

"Go away, all of you," ordered Felicity.

She went out with the nurse and left them standing there, looking at one another blankly.

"What's up?" asked Garrison querulously. "I had an appointment. . . ."

"Her husband is ill," Peter explained briefly, and leaving Garrison to digest the information and impart it to his companion he got his hat and overcoat and left. In the public hallway, at the elevator door he ran into the Japanese.

"Do you know what happened, exactly?" he asked, detaining the man a moment.

The Japanese shrugged.

"The chauffeur say . . . maybe he lose his arm . . . if he live. . . ."

The dark face worked oddly and presently Peter was alone. He stepped into the elevator and went on downstairs. When he reached the curb, the Van Anden car had gone.

He went to the hospital the next day. They could give him no information. Doctor Van Anden, they said, was "holding his own." Mrs. Van Anden was with him.

Disturbed, he went back that evening about dinner time. In the room where he waited, hoping to see Felicity a moment, or to talk to Miss Ainsworth, Felicity's manager came to him, rushing in like a man distracted. They had met often. The little, alert Jew seized him by the shoulder.

"You have heard? My God, I am ruined! She won't go on. She says let the understudy take the part. Understudy! Nothing holds the play together but Hawthorne. Now she stays here, in the hospital, in the next room to him, huddled in a corner like a peasant woman. She won't listen to me. She won't listen to anyone."

He rushed off, fairly foaming at the mouth, a distraught man. Peter waited, uneasily. After a while he managed to get the attention of the reception nurse.

130

"I'd like so much to see . . . Mrs. Van Anden . . . or one of the nurses," he begged. "I . . . I'm an old friend."

"You might go up," the nurse told him after a doubtful moment. "Miss Ainsworth is there."

He went, wondering at his own temerity. He knocked and, no one answering, opened the door and entered. The room was full of flowers. Felicity sat in a low chair. She still wore the teagown, although Peter saw a suitcase packed with day clothes open on the narrow bed. She did not seem to recognize him. Her face was frozen. She was alone.

"I . . . I'm so terribly sorry," Peter stammered.

She wrenched her eyes from the door which was closed between her room and the next, and looked at him dully. After a moment she said strangely:

"I believe you are."

Then she was silent again. Peter stood by the hall door, awkwardly enough. He had nothing to say to this congealed figure of grief and terror. After a moment she stirred and looked at him again. She looked every year of her age . . . and ten more.

"I can't be bothered . . ." she said abruptly.

"I'm sorry . . ." said Peter again.

He was turning to go, when she called him. She had risen and took a step toward him.

"Good-by," she said, still in that curious voice. "Why don't you go back to wherever you came from, Peter? To some one who cares for you? That's all that matters, you know."

He was so astonished that he forgot the situation. He said, very blankly, as if he were a child:

"But . . . my future . . . my writing?"

She laughed, and her expression did not change. It was quite horrible.

"But you can't write," she told him gently, "didn't you know that?"

He stared at her uncomprehending.

"But . . . you said . . ."

She gestured slightly with her bloodless hands.

"What does it matter what I said? I've always said

things like that . . . to young people. I thought . . . it kept me young, too . . . to have them come to me . . . look up to me . . . hang on my words and my influence. Influence!" She laughed again, and as Peter drew back, a little chilled and frightened, she came closer and put her hand impersonally on his shoulder.

"Do you know," she whispered, "they say that perhaps he won't live? He's lost his arm, won't want to live . . . now. He was a very great surgeon." Her voice was like an obituary. "But I'll take him away," she went on, "somewhere . . . anywhere . . . out of this . . . and . . . perhaps he'll forget. . . ."

The door between the rooms opened while Peter was still staring at her. A nurse appeared, and beckoned. Her voice was soft and hope ran through it like a golden thread.

"He's conscious . . . he's asking for you. . . ."

Peter saw Felicity turn at that, take a step, stumble, recover herself and run through the connecting door.

The door shut. He was alone, then, staring blindly at the flowers and the cool whiteness of the hospital room.

Miss Ainsworth came in from the hall where she had been talking to one of the staff surgeons. She had been crying, he noted, wondering why it moved him that she should cry.

"He'll live," she told him eagerly, not recognizing him and not caring.

"But his career?"

She flung him a scornful glance.

"He'll live, I said . . . I didn't say he'd care to."

Peter found himself walking down the long corridor with its hushed yet echoing air, the hospital smells, sickly yet cleanly, all about him, the nurses slipping past on their rubber soled shoes. When he reached the main floor Abrahams, the manager, was there again. He appeared to have rushed out only to rush in again, he had seen Peter passing the waiting room.

"You saw her?"

"Yes. . . . Van Anden had his arm amputated . . . but he'll live, they say."

Abrahams was not natively callous. He was a good

132

soul, a devoted husband, and father. But Van Anden meant less than nothing to him. He brushed aside the news.

"But . . . Felicity . . . you saw her?"

"She won't play," said Peter, eyeing him with a scornful pity.

Abrahams tossed his hands into the air, palms up.

"Then she's done for. *Kaput!* The understudy goes on, the piece closes. It's been hard enough as it is, the public is beginning to tire of her. If she retires for a time, she'll never come back."

"Perhaps she doesn't want to," suggested Peter, and left the little man staring.

He reached home. Laff was out. Peter sat down, filled a pipe and tried to think.

So he couldn't write! Well, he'd suspected it for some time. Oh, he'd talent, a trick of phrase—but it wasn't enough. And once he'd had ardor and an unflawed belief in himself. But no longer.

"Go back," Felicity had said, "to some one who cares. . . ."

No one had ever cared except Dolores.

He was suddenly sick with loneliness for her. He'd find her, make her talk things out. Marriage . . . marriage meant more than he had ever dreamed. It put out roots, grew tenaciously, held to life. You couldn't tear it up with hasty words. You couldn't destroy it by courts or the scratch of a pen.

He could go to Florida and see if she had reached the same conclusion. Laff's father owned a paper down there. He'd ask Laff to give him a letter.

The next day, after a sleepless night during which Laff did not come home, Peter telephoned Gaines. Gaines, they told him, was out of town, but they expected to hear from him during the day. If Peter's business was very important no doubt Mr. Gaines would get in touch with him.

He wrote a note to Mason, packed a bag, made his arrangements with an astonished Laff who lounged in about noon, and waited to see if he could hear from Gaines. Late in the afternoon the telephone rang.

The connection was bad and Peter strained his ears to

hear. He shouted across the miles of wire that he was going to Florida and any new move in the case could be communicated to him there, at Mrs. Comstock's address. He thought he heard Gaines exclaim, thin as the hum of an insect:

"I tried to get you yesterday," Gaines called dimly, "I saw Eldredge. In my opinion he does not intend to sign the papers. He hasn't said so officially but it looks that way. You'd better get in touch with him. If he refuses outright, we can talk divorce."

After a moment Peter hung up and stood thinking. So Eldredge had decided not to annul the marriage. His head whirled at the implication. He made no effort to think the thing out to its conclusion. He'd see Dolores first. If she were willing, they had another chance.

He picked up the receiver again and made reservations on the first train South.

CHAPTER XVII

ASTA said, a little breathlessly, one morning:

"I've succumbed to the current madness. . . ."

"What, exactly?"

"Real estate . . . on a shoe string. Don't look so worried, Dolores, I see all your cautious New England ancestors in your face! Do you remember a man named Ames, who motored up from Miami and had tea here? He knew Eva and Bert well, was disappointed not to find them. He had, he said, a surefire proposition in which he hoped to interest them. Failing them, he interested me, instead. I looked over my savings account and told him to go ahead. He's wired. I think I'll go down and see for myself. He says he has a buyer for this piece of land upon which I appear to have an option. Do you think you could manage alone . . . until to-morrow? There will be just the tea crowd, and it is thinning. The season is on the wane. The Evans will give me a lift. They are motoring to Miami for luncheon. I'll be back to-morrow. Incidentally if the town is as occupied by the real estate invasion as we hear, I might see about making arrangements to have *The Sailfish* moved down. We could stay on until it grows too hot. Do you mind, then, if I leave you, over night?"

"No. . . . Asta, do you think you'll make a lot of money?"

"I always think so . . . and I never do," the older woman laughed, "but once to everyone there must come a lucky break. . . . I believe Ames is trustworthy . . . not that I haven't been beguiled by an open countenance and a ready flow of salesmanship before. But I've always been a gambler. What it has cost me in self-control to keep from Bradley's no one will ever know! I sometimes wonder if my love of a wheel's turn or the fall of the dice will . . . lead me into matrimony . . . again."

"Matrimony!"

"Boris . . ." explained Asta, smiling faintly, "don't look so shocked Dolores . . . he can play the heart out of my breast."

Dolores was silent. She knew, having listened to his playing.

Asta departed. Dolores was alone with Alma until the tea-trade came. She was busy then when Sterling lounged across the deck, the dog beside him. She went to him presently and stood beside him at the rail.

"No tea?"

"None, I have an engagement, and I am late. You look a little tired. Now, why?"

She shook her head and the dark shining hair swung out over her ears.

"I'm not really. But I'm alone. Asta has gone to Miami until to-morrow."

"I see." He was silent a moment, his fine blond brows drawn. Then:

"I wish we might dine together," he said, "but Mrs. Redding is leaving . . . there's a farewell dinner. Listen . . . would you care to adventure a little? I'd call for you, about eleven, and we would drop in at the Beach Club and watch the play. And then, have supper?"

He looked at her intently, marked how she hesitated.

"Say yes!"

"Very well," Dolores agreed, on a sudden impulse, "I'll be ready."

"Wear the moonlight-and-lace," he urged her, and abruptly walked away.

When the last of the tea drinkers had gone and she and Alma had cleared away and had their supper, and Alma was ready to go across the bridge to her home across the Lake, the pleasant colored woman asked her anxiously:

"You want me to stay with you to-night? Miss Dolores, I don't like to leave you alone. . . ."

"That's all right," Dolores told her, "I don't mind. And I'm very near people, Alma, the apartments over the shop and all. But thanks just the same."

After Alma had gone she lay down on the couch in the "living room" to rest a little before she bathed and dressed. She wondered, uneasily, what Asta would say to this projected supper party? Nothing definite, probably . . . yet . . . she might not approve. But what of it? She, Dolores, wasn't a child, but a grown woman. She had been . . . no, she *was* married.

That sent her thoughts to a wire she had received the day before from Gaines. She had puzzled about it ever since, saying nothing to Asta. It was a day message and began by saying that the sender feared he had not been able to make Mr. Comstock understand that there was strong reason to believe that judicial opinion was antagonistic to their case, and that she and Mr. Comstock would do well to talk over what would be their next step.

That meant, as far as she could see, that Judge Eldredge had refused to sign the annulment papers. It meant that when she returned to town she must see Peter and find out what they would do next; and further—that she and Peter were still married and, unless they decided upon divorce, must remain so. But what did Gaines mean by saying he feared Peter had not understood? She could only believe that Peter had been unwilling to understand.

Ever since the wire came she had had to fight a feeling of relief, almost of happiness, and certainly of a security . . . which she had not felt since she left the uptown apartment.

She wondered, lying there, what Kay Sterling would say if he knew that legally, at any rate, she was not separated from Peter.

Kay Sterling interested her. She admitted it. She had seen him many times since the evening when, wheeling back from the Everglades, he had taken her hand in his own and said, "That's enough to go on" when she had

137

told him that she liked him. He had not touched her since. To-night? She wondered.

She envied him. He went everywhere, knew every one. He had money, culture, charm . . . and he was free. There was, she supposed, vaguely, no complete freedom without money.

After a long time during which she lay on the couch, without moving, her hands behind her head and her slim ankles crossed, she rose to dress. The sight of herself in the "moonlight-and-lace" gown gave her a throb of conscious pleasure, a feeling of power and carelessness.

He came at eleven, and they went to the Beach Club. Walking through the hall to the gaming rooms she saw herself reflected in mirrors, and in the eyes of passing men. She lifted her small, nobly shaped head, and a flush of excitement rose to where the crescents of black hair lay like curving wings on her cheeks.

The tables were crowded. Sterling said, smiling:

"You won't be tempted?"

"No. . . ."

"Well—suppose I risk something—for you? No? Well, for me, then? I think you'll bring me luck."

Someone rose from a roulette table and Sterling took his place, nodding to the croupier. Chips appeared. Dolores stood behind him, leaning forward to watch. The fascination of the game, the whirring wheel, the people, held her. Directly opposite a very small woman with a beautiful dead face was playing furiously. Her neighbor was a big man, saturnine and Semitic. Dolores knew who they were, everyone did. The woman's chips were soon exhausted and she reached out and took some of her neighbor's. His face did not change as she staked and lost them. At another table Dolores saw his wife playing quietly, a big, handsome woman with a brooding face and magnificent jewels.

Sterling was playing, whistling under his breath. He staked and won. The chips grew to a great pile. The women at his table began to follow his plays with their own. He was "in luck" they said.

The room was quiet, it was cool, the lights were not too

bright. Stage women, young and lovely, polo players, idlers, wives, divorced wives, quite young girls . . . elderly men . . . and here and there someone in day clothes, who was leaving by the late train, from the West Palm Beach side. The jewels in the rooms were worth millions.

Sterling won steadily. Then he grew careless. The tide turned and he lost. Dolores touched his sleeve. Two instincts warred within her; the instinct to be quiet, to watch, to reach out herself and put some of those harmless looking chips on a number; and the other to make him stop, before he lost all he had won.

"Do stop!" she implored him.

"Oh, not yet. It wouldn't be courteous!"

Eventually he cashed in, having broken exactly even. They walked out together and found that it was raining.

"My dress!" exclaimed Dolores in despair.

"But you'll be sheltered."

"Do you mind if we stop at the boat?" she urged him. "It may rain harder. . . . I'll get a wrap there. . . ."

"Very well. Tell me where it is and I'll get it. You stay in the chair."

He gave the order and they went to the dock. Sterling went aboard and found his way to Dolores' room. Her things were strewn about, untidy, rather charming. He stood there a minute, half frowning and half smiling. Then he caught up a cape from a hook in the wall, a dark voluminous affair, rubberized, and brought it back.

"Is this it?"

"Yes, my bathing cape. . . . I had nothing else but my mantilla," she said and laughed as he put it around her. It had seen service, smelled faintly of salt and Dolores exclaimed as a shower of sand fell from its folds, brushing her bare throat:

"Where are we going?"

"To my house. I ordered supper there," he told her evenly.

She was silent. She wanted to say . . . but . . . should I? and did not. He would laugh at her. Besides he was always calling her . . . "unsophisticated" and "infant"

139

. . . treating her as if she were a child. She shrugged and said nothing.

The house was up the Trail, set back in a garden. It was like a number of the houses only more beautiful than the majority, very Spanish in feeling. There was a patio and a fountain and trees sighing. Dolores had been there before, with Asta, for dinner.

The living room which they entered presently ran up two stories and the bedrooms opened from a balcony. Over the balcony a very marvellous Spanish shawl hung, red roses on black silk.

"You can find your way upstairs?" he asked her.

She knew the room to which she and Asta had gone before. She went up the stairs and once turned and looked at him. He was standing in the great room before a stone fireplace, smoking thoughtfully.

The room was lovely. An unscreened balcony opened from it, vines grew and twisted to the very railings. The room was big and the furniture Spanish—the coloring subdued save where the silken cushions on the great carven bed were bright as a flower garden.

She looked in a mirror, powdered her nose, burying her face in the ribbon-tied wisp of cotton to which the powder clung. Her eyes were darkly bright and her lips burned red.

Leaving the cape, she went downstairs again. The supper table was laid on a screened porch, where pots of flowers stood on the tiled floor and a rosy light burned, swinging from the ceiling.

One servant, a correct and wooden Englishman, waited on them and when he had been dismissed Sterling lifted his glass toward Dolores and watched the wine break into agitated dewdrops against the rim.

"Thank you for coming," he said.

When they had eaten they went into the living room. Dolores had taken a glass of champagne. She rarely drank anything and now she could feel the warm sunlight of the wine, light and dry, singing in her veins. She commented, motioning toward the piano:

"I didn't know you played."

"I sing," he explained astonishingly, "for my own

amusement, and play enough for my accompaniments. Go over there and lie down and I shall 'demonstrate.' "

He motioned toward an immense divan. Obediently she lay back against the cushions and watched him curiously. He sat down at the piano, in profile, fingered the keys gently as if feeling his way, his head flung back to keep the smoke of his cigarette out of his eyes, and his eyelids half closed. Then he flung the cigarette in the nearby fireplace and, still touching the keys with that extraordinary gentleness, sang.

Dolores trembled. His voice was magnificent . . . a dark, somber baritone in which a strange tortured heart seemed to pulse and beat and struggle toward assuagement or release. Some of the songs she recognized . . . one or two of the Heine *Lieder*, a French song she'd heard somewhere, and something vaguely familiar, Oriental.

Presently the voice ceased and the piano spoke again, as if in reluctant farewell. And then he came over and sat down beside her.

"Oh . . . *don't* stop . . ." she begged.

"Enough. I don't do that often," he told her.

"But your voice! To . . . to hide it from people!" she reproached him.

He shrugged, smiling:

"I keep it to amuse myself . . . that is all. You cannot picture me upon the stage can you, in war paint and feathers?"

She could not, and said so. Across the room a clock ticked, warningly. She could hear the fountain singing in the patio.

"I must go. . . ."

"Not yet. . . ." He leaned forward, took her hands, "Dolores—that's such a lovely name, dear—sorrowful and passionate. . . . I love you, . . . you must have known."

She let her hands lie in his, sat upright, facing him, the color drained from her face.

"Will you trust yourself to me?"

She answered, whispering:

"I can't. I can't marry anyone."

"Not marriage," he spoke gently, almost sadly, "I

141

couldn't marry you dear, even if I were willing to clip those exquisite wings of yours. . . . I'm not free."

"But you said . . ." she began, bewildered.

"Oh, free, . . . yes . . . in that sense. I was married, as I told you. I am separated. But she still has the right to my name. She will not divorce me in any circumstances. Nor do I wish her to. What difference would it make?"

Dolores asked slowly:

"You're not . . . offering marriage then."

"No. Love. Freedom. Everything money can buy you. I demand nothing but your kindness," he said, somberly. "You shall go where you please, live where you wish and afford me in return a little tenderness, something of your glowing youth. Do you care . . . enough? Such caring takes courage. I shall protect you . . . as much as possible."

She said, in a little voice,

"I . . . never believed in marriage, you know. . . . Never."

Kay Sterling answered, watching her, showing no astonishment,

"No. Why should you? I would not bind you, darling."

Abruptly he had her in his arms. She made one frightened gesture, a motion of rebellion.

She was rigid, quiet. The room swayed about her. Her senses seemed sharpened, alert. She heard the clock ticking; she heard the fountain; she remembered an echo of song. The one thing that had no meaning was his voice speaking to her urgently.

Now his mouth lay upon her own.

Suddenly, she wrenched herself free and regarded him wildly. She caught the back of one hand to her bruised lips and her eyes filled with tears, slow drops of crystal. He looked at her, his face changing. He seemed older, menacing, he was ashen and his eyes had burned to a color that was clear, amazing green.

"Dolores!"

She shook her head, violently.

"No! *No!*"

She knew now. Love and Freedom. But there was no freedom where love was not. She did not love this man.

He was a terrifying stranger who had kissed her. This spell had died, as the songs had perished in the echoing air, as the bright compulsion of the wine had vanished from her veins. Her heart beat thickly, with pure terror. She sprang to her feet, startled and graceful as a woodland creature.

"Let me go!"

He rose, very quiet, a little ugly.

"And what have I done?" he asked her.

"Everything. I don't love you. I don't want you!" she answered with a stark, compelling simplicity.

Suspicion took him. Had he been . . . mistaken? Was she playing for the bigger stakes, the stake he pretended to belittle, which he was not prepared to yield again to any woman, no matter how desirable?

He asked, low:

"You do not care . . . at all?"

"No." He came toward her and she retreated, shrinking. "Don't touch me . . . don't touch me!" she stammered.

He smiled, mirthlessly.

"I . . . revolt you?"

"Yes," she told him with the utter honesty of terror, "not before. I didn't know. I was a fool. I know now."

He was stabbed to the quick and showed it. He asked, still smiling, still softly:

"Why do you let me buy your dresses?"

"Dresses?"

"Dress, then. Surely you were not quite as innocent . . . ? Your heart was set on the thing. I made an arrangement . . . with the shop."

"Oh . . . *oh!*"

She looked into his eyes, flushed darkly red and turned, running lightly up the stairs, her high heels clicking out their little tune of flight. He reached to an ivory, carven box, took out a cigarette and lighted it. He made no motion to follow, merely moved to the foot of the stairs and stood there smoking, smiling with hard lips.

Dolores raced into the room where she had left her cape . . . how many hours before? She saw herself in the mirror, scarlet cheeked, dishevelled, her mouth shaken and outraged. A gust of temper took and harried her. She

143

lifted her strong young hands and tore the dress from her. "It's worth any price you paid for it," he had told her.

She would not pay . . . more. He might have the dress.

Tall and lovely, she stood there momently, her skin like cream and the rose-white flesh of fruit, her body clothed in a wisp of lingerie and a scant short slip. She snatched up the cape and flung it about her, drawing it close, the hood over her hair. It covered her to the ankles. And she stood there a second, her eyes desperate.

She could not face him.

She ran to the open balcony. The rain fell, cooling her hot cheeks. She looked over and saw a wooden pergola beneath her covered with strong vines. Without any hesitation she swung herself from the railing, reached for a foothold, found it, and clambered to the ground.

While Sterling waited, implacable and patient, ready to lash her with his tongue and send her home, and never see her again, she was creeping around the side of the house to the Trail. It was very late. She was not likely to meet people, save a few belated homecomers.

Upstairs in the bedroom the lights burned and a dress lay torn upon the floor, a dress of black lace and metallic cloth with one half opened flower.

Reaching the path panic was at her heels, abruptly. Suppose he followed . . . or the dog? She began to run, blindly. It was raining hard. She clutched the cape about her, running, running. . . .

Could she reach the house boat before he knew she had gone?

A man came out of a side path and walked up the Trail, his raincoat collar turned up, his hat pulled low. He was too late to step aside and she ran directly into him, crying out with terror at the contact.

He caught her, steadied her, and opened his lips to say something reassuring. Light was dimly on the path here where their trails converged.

"Dolores!"

She looked up into his face. She was long past astonishment. It was Peter.

CHAPTER XVIII

FOR a full minute they stared at one another. Only the palm trees spoke, swinging to the wind with a brittle sound as the rain beat like toy musketry upon the fronds. The Lake murmured on the shore, and lights showed from boats at anchor.

"Peter!"

She took his arm in her two hands and asked wonderingly:

"You're . . . *real?*"

"Very much so." He tried to laugh, failing, "But we mustn't stand here, you'll be soaked. I've been to the houseboat, no one was there. I began to think it was the wrong place."

They turned, walking toward the dock. She answered, half out of dreams:

"Asta is away over night."

When they reached the boat and went below she remembered her half-clad condition and drew the cape closely about her. Peter mustn't see. . . .

But he saw the vivid blush which flooded her face and misinterpreted it.

"Wait a minute," she stammered. . . . "I'll be right back. . . ."

While she was absent he wandered about the room, looking at the gift-display, not really seeing it.

When she came back, wearing a working smock, her hair brushed smoothly, he held one of Eva's panels in his hands and was examining it. Yet he was not aware that it represented a palm tree against a sunset. His heart shook so that his sight was dim. He put down the picture and said abruptly:

"You've bobbed your hair!"

"Yes. . . . Peter, sit down. What are you doing here?"

He thought she looked frightened. But it was not fright which held her but a sense of unreality. She had been hurried from emotion to emotion with such velocity in the last few hours that she scarcely knew what possessed substance and what did not.

He sat down and laughed, uneasily.

"I was restless. Laff . . . the fellow I roomed with . . . gave me a letter to a West Palm Beach paper owned by his father. I got in this morning and went to the office. I had to hang around waiting for the editor. They didn't take me definitely, but said they might give me a try, and to come back to-morrow. I crossed the bridge late to-night and looked for you. You weren't here. I've been wandering around ever since, even down to the big fishing piers."

Silence fell betwen them. He was in an agony of uncertainty. Should he tell her now . . . bluntly. . . . How would she take it? He found himself, saying, instead, breathlessly:

"I liked the long hair better . . . but you're more beautiful than ever, Dolores."

He rose, pulled a footstool near her and sat down, his hands clasped about his knees.

"I didn't tell you all the truth. I came because you were here."

She didn't answer. He thought her face hardened against him. He explained.

"I wanted to talk things over quietly. We've never done so. We made an utter mess of it. I can't see why . . . exactly . . . and now that things are ended . . ."

She exclaimed and he looked up sharply. He had meant to go on to say "now that the annulment is out of the question . . ." but he did not, her exclamation halted him.

She had cried out because it had come to her suddenly

146

what he meant . . . and what Gaines had meant in the wire. Gaines hadn't, for some reason, been able to make Peter understand. Peter thought that the papers were signed, he said "now that things are ended. . . ." He believed they were . . . free. That was why, she thought, her heart heavy, his eyes shone so, with the old light of excitement, of happiness. And she'd have to tell him.

But she couldn't. Instead she asked, feeling her way: "You talked to Mr. Gaines?"

"Yes," he answered, puzzled, "but by telephone. It was long distance, I couldn't get the details. . . ."

He hesitated again, looking at her. She was the color of a rose and her lips shook. Peter thought, the situation suddenly clear as sunlight to him . . . she believes I've come to tell her the annulment is accomplished . . . that's why she's so happy.

Dolores was thinking desperately. If she told him the truth, if she showed him the wire, he would leave her. And she knew as well as she had ever known anything, that she could not endure to have him leave her. He belonged to her. She had denied herself, but it was true. If they could start afresh, if they could learn happiness, then it wouldn't matter . . . she could tell him his mistake . . . and he'd laugh at it. But not now. She couldn't risk losing him. The most terrible temptation of her life assailed her. Suppose she left him in ignorance, allowed him to think himself free? She asked, stammering, wanting to be sure:

"Then we're not married any more?"

Peter's heart twisted with pain. He looked at her a moment before answering. She was so dear, she was within the reach of his hand. If he told her the truth she would send him away, he might never see her again except in Gaines' office. He thought wildly . . . if I let her believe herself free . . . perhaps she'll talk it out with me . . . perhaps I can make her *see*.

Aware that he was taking a tremendous risk, aware that he was branding himself a liar and that one day she would find him out, he answered, evading the direct negative:

"Perhaps we never were . . . really."

Dolores was silent. His gray eyes, fixed upon hers, had

darkened. His head was so close she could have reached out to touch the thick rusty brown hair. She folded one hand in the other and waited, her face colorless.

"Dolores . . . the ceremony couldn't marry us. What was wrong? We started out with such high hearts, and so much love?"

Now, because he believed himself free he was speaking to her from his soul, she thought. She made a sound like a sob.

"I know, Peter . . . what happened?"

"We were kids," he muttered, "crazy kids. . . ."

After a time she asked, gently:

"And your work, Peter?"

He lifted his head and looked at her with a smile which tore her heart.

"I've given it up. I can't write."

"You can!"

"No, dear," he contradicted quietly.

She asked, timidly:

"But . . . Miss Hawthorne?"

"She's had a tragic time, Dolores. Her husband, the surgeon, has lost his arm. The last word I had he was expected to live but his career is smashed. She's not going back to the stage. It doesn't seem to matter to her," he mused . . . "his career or her own . . . as long as they have each other."

"It wouldn't," said Dolores.

He looked at her a moment. She was right. Nothing mattered as long as you had the Beloved. If his resolution had faltered at what he believed was his deception it hardened now. Then his eyes narrowed and he asked, abruptly:

"When we met . . . why were you running?"

"I was afraid."

"You?"

"I've been afraid so often, Peter. Didn't you know that?" she asked him oddly.

But he only countered frowning:

"But . . . to-night?"

"It was a man, Peter," she explained, gravely. "I'd been to supper at his house, and I ran away."

He arose, overturning the footstool:

"Dolores!"

He took her hands, drew her to her feet.

"He didn't . . . hurt you? Who was he. . . . Oh, my God," said Peter simply, "it's all been my fault."

"No. He didn't hurt me. I won't tell you who he was. He doesn't matter. It was when I found out that he didn't matter that I was afraid . . . and ran. I've always run away. I ran away from our beautiful plans and our hopes. I ran away from—marriage—from you."

Abruptly she bowed her head on his shoulder and cried bitterly. He held her, as she had been held many times, as he had since dreamed he would hold her again.

"Darling, you're safe," he said.

"I know . . ."

Presently they sat on the couch, handfast, and smiled at each other, shyly, as children smile who have kissed and made up.

"It's always been you, Dolores. I've loved you always, even when I seemed not to. I love you now . . . I've missed you damnably."

He leaned to her offered lips and the pressure of his mouth on hers was beauty and pain and benediction.

"You're mine . . ." he told her unsteadily, "I'll not let you go."

"I've never been anything but yours. . . ."

He said again humbly:

"It was my fault. I was eaten with egotism. I fancied it was freedom I wanted. But I didn't allow you yours. I wanted to be free, but I wanted you bound to me."

He broke off. Now, if ever, was the time to explain, to tell the truth, now that he had her acknowledgement. Now that their love shone clear between them. Yet he dared not risk telling her . . . not now. . . . Later he thought, taking a coward's refuge.

It was then that Dolores took the definite step. If Peter believed that he held his freedom in his hands and his love in his arms, let him think it. Later . . . she would tell him.

149

Perhaps, when she told him he would no longer want . . the freedom.

She sprang to her feet, a laughing flame.

"It's all different now," she cried, "I ran away from you once. But before that, I ran away with you. Let's run away again . . . together."

"What do you mean?" he asked, staring, but his heart beat hotly. For he knew what she meant. If he permitted her . . . her playtime, her self-deception, might he not win her to himself forever? Might he not lead her to see that marriage was of the soul, and freedom of the spirit.

"I mean, just that. . . . Begin at the beginning. Start at the crossroads again. . . ."

He rose, swung her into his arms.

"You'd dare?"

"Anything . . . with you!"

He found her pitifully lovely in what he believed to be her mistaken gallantry.

"Sit down . . . I want to look at you!"

She perched on the arm of a chair, leaning toward him. He dropped to his knees, and put his arms about her waist and turned his face to hers.

"And you wouldn't be afraid . . . this time?"

"Never afraid with you," she said.

Now they were children, back in a garden swing, with peach blossoms drifting past, and a spring wind calling. They were children playing hide and seek, playing make-believe, and touched with a heart-breaking lunacy.

After a time he reflected,

"Damn the job! We'll get a second hand flivver and a camping outfit. I know where there's one to be had, some stranded tin canner left it and went back to the farm. I'll buy up the whole works in the morning and we'll go gypsying."

"It's almost morning now," she reminded him.

They went up on deck. It was not raining, the sky was bathed in the pale ruby light of dawn. They found dry camp stools and sat down to watch the sun rise, to see the light shoot like a golden arrow across the stirring Lake.

"Good morning, Peter."

Two solemn runaways, they leaned and kissed there, in the dawn.

"Alma comes early," she said. stirring, "she's the woman who helps us here. Let's have coffee before she comes. I can really make coffee now, Peter. Then I'll pack and we'll go buy the flivver. I'll leave word for Asta. . . . Poor Asta," she sighed, not caring much, "she'll be so angry."

They went below and Dolores made coffee that was nectar and toast that was ambrosia. And the sun rose higher over the water and laughed at them.

Then, while he cleared away the breakfast things, whistling, she pulled out a suitcase and flung some necessities in it. Calling him to lock it for her, she sat down at the desk and wrote to Asta.

"Peter came," she wrote, "and I've run away with him. We're going to start all over again. Asta, forgive me, and wish us luck. It's dreadful to leave you alone like this . . . but I can't help going. And thank you, dear Asta, for all you've done for me. I'm awfully happy. If when you leave you send my things over to Alma's I could pick them up there. . . ."

"I'm ready," she announced presently, joining Peter, "I've left word for Alma too."

There were no chair-boys at that hour. They walked over the bridge together in the brilliant sunlight.

Before noon Peter had expended some of his savings and acquired the flivver, the camping outfit and a cap. Dolores went to a shop which was just opening and was supplied with breeches, boots and khaki shirts by an uninterested store keeper.

Then she went back to where Peter waited.

"I've written to the paper," he told her, gravely, "I resigned, before I was hired."

During their wait in the garage where the flivver was refurbished, Dolores suggested, appealingly:

"I've some money too, Peter, if you need it."

He frowned, and started to speak. She whispered, for the garage helpers stood nearby:

"We're . . . just partners now."

151

He laughed at that and caught her hand so hard that it hurt.

"Bless you. . . ."

Presently they trundled out of the garage. The mechanic and his helper stood grinning, wiping oily hands on cotton waste.

"Honeymooners," deduced one of them, wisely.

Driving out of town, they turned north. The wind was in their faces, the sun shone on them. The flivver rattled along bravely.

Back on *The Gilded Sailfish* Asta was reading Dolores' note. She sat a moment in thought, then smiled:

"Mad children . . ." she said aloud.

CHAPTER XIX

FORTY or fifty miles north of West Palm Beach they came upon a small frame-and-varnish fishing Inn set directly on a long strip of sand. There were a few scattered cottages and an enormous sense of peace. It seemed a thousand miles removed from Palm Beach and the colorful restless life of resorts. Dolores, when Peter had subdued the flivver to a standstill and suggested something to eat, looked about her and cried out, happily:

"Oh, Peter . . . let's stay here!"

The Inn was empty. They had a simple meal in a deserted dining room and Peter went to consult the proprietor. Was there, he wanted to know, any place where they might camp for a few days?

The host was desolate that his rooms were not wanted. But he was a genial soul and it was the end of the season. He fancied these touring youngsters, who in no way resembled the usual tin-canners, would soon tire of their bargain and come to him for a Christian bed and bath. He pondered a moment.

"There's the Point," he told Peter, "you might camp there."

"But would the owners object?"

"I shouldn't think so. The Point belonged to two Northern gentlemen, they have come down every season for years, for the fishing. I never saw either of them in anything but bathing suits, except at dinner time," the landlord replied, "but they're not down this year. Mr. Carson

153

died last summer, and Mr. Jackson hadn't the heart to come, he wrote me. I'm official caretaker. I see no reason why you shouldn't put up there as long as you wish. You can get supplies from me, and if you grow tired of a frying pan you can come over for meals. There won't be many mosquitoes to bother you, even later, for the breeze is strong enough to blow them away."

So they went with their guide to inspect the Point. It was a long jut of land running into the water . . . upon one side was the ocean, upon the other an inlet, forming a small, quiet bay. It was colored like a lithograph, strong, blinding colors. The beach was so white that it dazzled, water and sky so blue they seemed unreal. There were trees, and a rustic shelter where the owners had their meals. In one place in the sand there were flat stones in a hollow where they learned the fishers had cooked their catch over a charcoal fire.

Over the beach and through the trees the wind sang, cool and bracing. It seemed to Dolores that she could almost see it, a living presence, tinted blue by sky and water and golden by the sun.

"It's heavenly . . ." she told Peter.

He nodded, holding her hand tight. Quiet, and the sea, and wind, the sun warmed sand, and the dear loneliness of two. . . .

After carrying the things from the flivver they made camp with the help of a lank young man who did odd jobs about the Inn, and who offered them his flat-bottomed motor boat for a day's fishing, at an unseasonal price, any time they wished it. By the time the best site was chosen for the tent, and their few possessions in place, they were healthily and happily tired and went to the Inn for supper, and to see the car safely in the garage. When they escaped from the landlord and his motherly wife it was late, and reaching the Point by the narrow trail through the trees they saw a great moon rising, flooding the dark shadows and shining glamourously on the beach.

They went to the beach and sat down and looked out upon the moving mystery of the waters, and listened to the crying of the wind which was like a great gray bird flying among the trees.

"Are you happy, Dolores?"

"Yes. . . ."

After a time she said slowly:

"It seems so strange . . . yesterday . . . I never dreamed of this. And now . . ."

"And now?"

"Oh, I don't know. Peter, are we a little mad? See how we do everything on . . . on the spur of the moment? Running away that first time together . . . and then running away from each other . . . and now, again. With hardly a word spoken, just making up our minds and going. Do you think we're sane, Peter?"

"No," he told her frankly, "I don't. And it doesn't matter, does it? Do you *want* to be sane again . . . after a lunacy like this?"

She was silent, lying back in his arms. But they would have to be sane again. She was realizing that more and more. With every day that passed the reckoning drew nearer. Would he forgive her? She thought, defiantly . . . it won't matter. I've had this. . . .

So she reached up and kissed him. Presently, enchanted children, they walked back to the tent and went inside together.

Time passes swiftly in Eden. Dolores grew rosy brown, Peter was tanned copper colored. They spent much time in the chore-boy's boat, coming in shore to swim and to cook their morning's catch. Occasionally they "dressed" and went to the Inn for a meal. And they talked, incessantly as never before. No one bothered them, there were no disturbances. There were not even duties to distract them, they admitted, rejoicing shamelessly in idleness. No office for Peter, no housekeeping for Dolores. When they had eaten they buried the scraps and threw the paper plates into a heap and had a nice, clean bonfire.

It seemed to them they had never known one another before, not even when they were children, swinging in an old orchard, dreaming their glowing, impossible dreams.

Each was a little frightened, hiding it from the other. Is

155

it, asked Peter, because she believes herself free that she is willing to reveal herself to me? And her thoughts and fear ran shoulder to shoulder with his own.

But neither dared to speak . . . and imperil the enchantment.

During this time he told her about Felicity.

"I was never in love with her, not for a moment. She fascinated me. She seemed so—remote. And she flattered me, made me think that with her help I could be a great man." He laughed, without bitterness. "Well, I know now. When we go back I'll get a job on a paper again. I wasn't even a good reporter, my head was so turned. I scorned the grind, looked on it as a stepping stone only. I'll work, really, next time."

He stopped. He hadn't meant to say anything about "going back." When they went back, she would have to know. He looked at her, afraid she would go on with the subject. But she was silent. It dropped between them like a stone.

During this period of their lives she told him about Sterling, keeping from him only the shame and terror of the scene in his house that night, and the method of her escape.

"I was so lonely for you," she explained, "it was at my heart all the time. And he was charming. It was all vanity, I suppose. But when he . . . touched me . . . I awoke. I knew there couldn't be anyone but you Peter, as long as I lived."

They were taking a siesta, lying on the beach in their bathing suits. Peter flung out an arm and touched her hand.

"I'm trying to be sensible about that episode," he told her, "but it's damned hard. My instinct is to find the man and kill him. . . ."

"Darling, don't be melodramatic. He isn't worth killing. It wasn't his fault. I was a fool. And a man has a right to think anything he pleases of a fool and her folly."

Upon another occasion he told her about Marise.

"She was like you, somewhat. She hadn't your fineness and your wonder, but she was dark and the way she moved her hands and her body reminded me . . . and she frightened me. She kept telephoning. There was no attraction

156

for me save the chance resemblance, and at first I didn't go to see her. Then, once I went. It was pretty awful. There was a moment when I thought . . . if I shut my eyes . . . and stopped my ears . . . I could imagine . . . but, I couldn't. So I went away . . . for good."

"I suppose I should hate her," Dolores mused, "but I don't. After all, she didn't let you forget. And even if she did attract you, well, it was through me, wasn't it? It was different with Felicity. I felt she was taking something that I'd never had . . . something of your mind and spirit."

"It's over," he told her, "forget them all. We know where we belong."

Dolores turned over on her back and clasped her hands behind her head.

"I must write Asta again, and some day, go to see Alma. I wonder if the boat has gone to Miami? Alma's people will know. I treated Asta badly, Peter. Why is it that in order to get our own way we have to wound someone? I've been thinking . . . Cousin Carolyn and Cousin Sarah . . . and your father, for instance. We haven't thought how hurt they've been."

"Sometimes," said Peter astonishingly, "I've thought I'd like to go back to the mills. They are incredibly behind the times. Had I been able to swallow my pride I might have gone . . . but I came for you instead. . . ."

She did not answer. Anything that touched on the future or the far past seemed to put her in jeopardy. She was forced, by her deception of him, to live in the present.

After some weeks at the Point the wanderlust seized them and they traveled North for a time, following the charm of the Indian River and going cross country as far as Tampa, near the Gulf. They took their time and were lazy and happy. There were few tourists in Florida now for the season was well over, the hot spring had come, and summer was not far ahead.

They knew, of course, and sometimes spoke of it, that it couldn't last. One day they must go back. So far, their joint resources were holding out. They had only their simple meals to provide and the car, for camping sites were free to them. But Peter, with an extremely practical

157

air, put aside the money for their fare home and sealed it in an envelope.

"I'd hate to walk," he told Dolores when she laughed at him for his precaution.

On their return to the Point from the longest trip they had yet taken they found Mr. Farlowe, the owner of the Inn, thinking of departure. The Inn was now closed to outsiders. He came over to the Point one day, and talked to Peter while Dolores sat outside the tent on a camp stool and did some necessary darning.

"You're welcome to stay as long as you want," said Farlowe, scratching his fringe of reddish hair. "Florida isn't as bad in the summer as people say. Not here, anyway, where there's always a good breeze. But, I've had a word from Mrs. Carson and Jackson . . . and they want to sell. They say they won't come down any more now that Carson's gone. Can't say as I blame 'em."

"Sell?"

"Yes . . . it's a pretty big tract you know, runs far back. I was thinking of advertising it for some millionaire's camp or other. But we're off the railroad and millionaires seem to like to make their camps at places like Palm Beach, and the real estate fellows are all for Miami and St. Petersburg, and the rest of the towns."

"I see," said Peter thoughtfully.

That night he woke Dolores suddenly and said, without warning:

"Dolores! If we could buy the Point . . . somehow? I have a hunch. I didn't tell Farlowe, but just that one day I was in West Palm, a chap came into the office and talked while I was hanging around. I didn't listen closely, but there was something about finding a place for a fishing club —half a dozen rich men. Of course if this place ever gets on the beaten track, it will be worth—lots of money."

"It will be spoiled then," she told him sleepily.

"I know. But—if we could swing it? We'd still have our fare back and something over . . . and I could sell the flivver for a few dollars. Suppose I take my quarterly income and savings and buy an option?"

"Take mine, too," Dolores said and slept profoundly.

A day or so later Peter approached Farlowe.

"Do you think the people who own the Point would let me have an option? I'd like to get it if I could. Would you be willing to wire them—you're the agent, aren't you? and see how much they'd take. Do you think it would be a very stiff price?"

Farlowe pondered. He liked Peter. He trusted him. He said, after a while:

"No, not as prices go. They're well off, and there isn't much chance of getting rid of the Point at a big profit. It's not laid out so it would be a good site for a settlement, and there's where the money is. There'd have to be so much spent on clearing. I'll wire."

Several days later Peter had a thirty-day option at two thousand dollars. It took all he and Dolores had. But they risked it. Farlowe who was certainly no business man accepted their checks in behalf of his principals and scraped up a lawyer from somewhere.

"Well," said Peter breathless, "we've done it. We'll be paupers—or millionaires before long. I'll go to West Palm and dig out that man I saw in the office again. I'll manage, Dolores, but I shouldn't have staked what you have."

"We're partners," she told him.

CHAPTER XX

AFTER hours spent in the offices of the Maynard newspaper Peter succeeded in finding out where he could reach the agent for the proposed fishing club. The man, it seemed, was temporarily in Miami. Peter telephoned Mr. Farlowe, and asked him to tell Dolores that he was off to Miami in the flivver, would buy a toothbrush and a clean collar en route and to expect him when she saw him again.

Dolores received the news placidly. How like Peter, she thought, hot on the trail, as happy as a child with a new toy, running down his very indefinite "prospect." Mrs. Farlowe urged her to come to the Inn for the night. But she would not. She stayed in the tent, had a cold supper and spent some hours on the beach before bedtime.

It was lonely without Peter. The water seemed as vast an expanse as the indifferent sky. The wind was like a whispered warning. Returning to the tent, she tried to sleep but every night-sound woke her. It was silly to be frightened, she argued, yet no amount of reasoning could make her less so. Strange, what a difference the one beloved presence made! The Point was far from a wilderness yet without Peter she felt lost in a deep forest, millions of miles from anyone.

But now that she was alone she had to face her thoughts. She was aware that soon this venture must draw to an end; that Peter would have to know. How much would he blame her? Would he hate her for deceiving him through silence? Would his pride be wounded; would he feel that he had been made a fool of? . . . Freedom! She had grown to hate the word. It meant nothing to her any more. Nothing mattered except Peter. If only she could make him see that their happiness hadn't depended on the pretense he believed in, but upon themselves and their love for one another.

Another thought came to her, as bitter as lonely tears. On the Tampa trip they had stopped at a fruit farm for water. The woman there was leather-faced and lean, with stooped shoulders and very young eyes. There were children around the ramshackle house, and a baby, swaddled around its fat middle but otherwise as Nature made it, rolled in the grass under a tree. While Peter attended to the car, Dolores talked to the woman, and played with the child, a brown urchin, socially inclined. She had never before felt the pull of laughing, self-willed weakness. The poor baby next door to her in the uptown flat had affected her with pity only, or irritation. But this infant seemed a part of sun and soil, it was round and friendly and healthy. And she had taken it in her arms and wondered what a child of Peter's and hers would be like.

They had been fools, she thought unhappily . . . talking about freedom and paying so many penalties and finding that freedom was a mirage. At least so she had found it, coming to believe that only the price you paid for your delusion was real.

Toward dawn she rose and went to the beach and sat there and watched the dawn. Presently, heavy-eyed from lack of sleep, she stripped off her gay pyjamas and swam out into the clear water which still held the chill of night. Now it was turning from gray to blue and she could swim far out in a golden rosy path, lithe and bronze-limbed and refreshed.

During the day Peter sent word that he had found his man and made an appointment but might not be back for another day or so.

The hours were interminable. Mrs. Farlowe sent her a message that she was driving to West Palm Beach to do some shopping. Would Dolores care to go?

Dolores welcomed the idea. She could see Alma and

161

hear news of Asta and the boat, she could collect her things. When she was dressed she looked about the camp. In the pocket of Peter's suitcase was the envelope with the fare home. She slipped it in her handbag. The camp was safe enough, she reflected, but she would be away for several hours and one never knew who might come.

She rode to the town in the back seat with Mrs. Farlowe while Farlowe drove. She had explained that she wished to find a woman who had been an old servant and named the address. After they had all lunched together Farlowe drove her to Alma's cottage on the outskirts, and said he would return for her within an hour or two.

Alma was in her backyard hanging up some startling looking garments. She turned in amazement as Dolores opened the gate and came in.

"For heaven's sake!" exclaimed Alma in her soft drawl.

She took Dolores into the house, casting a scornful look at the untidiness of the neighboring yards and houses. Born Carolinian, Alma had come with the Mantons their first season as cook, and had married one of the chair-boys. Her savings had built the house and during the summers she and her little family migrated north and found positions.

She brushed aside a small, clamouring pickaninny, and dusted a chair in the darkened sitting room.

"I'm right glad to see you, Miss Dolores . . . you're looking fine."

"Did Miss Karsten tell you why I left?"

Alma displayed superb teeth in a sympathetic grin.

"Sho' did . . . said yo' husband come for yo'."

"Was she angry, Alma?"

"No, not to say angry, exactly," Alma answered sitting down by the mission table which was her pride, and straightening the red cloth which covered it.

"Did the houseboat go to Miami?"

"No, Miss Dolores. Miss Karsten done went North. Mr. Manton sent a man down to look after the boat."

"Did you forward a letter from me to Miss Karsten?"

"Yes'm," Alma smote her black forehead. "Laws, I disremembered. They's mail for you . . . it come to the

162

houseboat and was sent hyer lak Miss Asta wanted. Miss Asta, too, she lef' a letter with me. She reckoned you'd come some day."

She went away and returned with a package of envelopes. Then she disappeared into the kitchen and Dolores heard her clattering cups and clanking stove lids. The black baby crept in and looked at the stranger with bright eyes, chuckled, and vanished.

Dolores opened Asta's letter first.

"I suppose you will go to Alma's some day, my dear," it read, "if you are still in Florida. As for your running away—it's your own life. I wish you'd waited the few hours until I came back, I might have advised you, although that isn't my usual role. I do wish you happiness. But, *be sure you are sure.* . . .

"The plan of moving the boat isn't feasible. As soon as I hear from the Mantons I'll go home. I made money on my deal, by the way. And I enclose a check, it covers what I owe you. For altho' you left without notice you could not have done so at a less awkward time, and this little sum is due you."

Dolores turned to the other letters, her mind distant. "Be sure you are sure," Asta had written. Well, she was sure. But when Peter found out how much would her certainty avail her? She felt a slow, unaccustomed flush of shame which burned through her whole body.

There were letters from home, rather plaintive. When was she returning to her husband? When was she coming back on a visit? The cousins had seen Ashabel Comstock, driving by. He had looked badly; they had heard he was not well. Peter's duty lay with his father. Why did not Dolores write more often?

The last letter was to Peter, in her care . . . and it was, by the letterhead, from Gaines.

Dolores went white. She weighed it in her hand, thinking. She had no right to open it. Yet it seemed to her that she was desperate, she must know what the lawyer had to say to Peter. She tore it open with shaking fingers and the first few lines stood out in letters like black flame . . .

"Thinking you didn't quite understand over the tele-

phone . . . I wired Mrs. Comstock. . . . It is definite now
. . . the case has gone against us, as I told her in my wire
I thought it would. Eldredge refuses to grant the annulment. . . . When you come back perhaps we can devise
another plan."

There was more but this was enough. She put the letter
back in the envelope, very carefully, and sat there with it
in her lap. When Peter read this, he would know . . . he
would also know that she had known all along.

She was sick with the temptation to tear the letter into
a thousand pieces. But to what purpose? she thought,
wearily. It would only put off the reckoning a few days
longer. She looked down dully and another sentence or
two caught her attention and held it . . . "there are ways
and means," wrote Gaines cheerfully, "divorce . . . another state. . . . I know how disappointed you will be that
the other plan failed and how much you desire your complete freedom."

So Gaines knew . . . how much Peter wished to be rid
of the tie which held him to her.

Shame took her again, wave after wave of it, like a
creeping nausea. She had been—terribly guilty. Her deception of Peter was without excuse. He would hate her.
All their happy time would go for nothing.

There was only one thing she could do, to make it up to
him. She must go away, at once; she must see Judge Eldredge and beg him on her knees to reconsider, to give
Peter the freedom he wanted. If she did that perhaps Peter
would forgive her.

Sitting there, she planned, rapidly, feverishly, and presently Alma came in with a cup of tea and some toast.

"It's early," said Alma, "but you'll want a bite before
yo' starts back. I made the cin-mon toast yo' all likes so
much. Fo' Gawd, Miss Dolores, what's the matter?"

She stared at the gray face of the girl who had not
looked up at her entrance.

"I've had bad news," Dolores explained with an effort,
"I must go North at once . . . to-night . . . I'll tell the
people who brought me . . . will you keep me here, Alma,
until the train goes?"

Alma took the cold hands between her warm palms.

"Honey, don' shake so . . . of co'se," she murmured soothingly.

She made Dolores drink the hot tea and then said practically:

"But you ain't dressed for travelin'?"

"It doesn't matter. . . ."

Alma thought a moment, then her good face cleared.

"They's that bag of you's here, and some other clothes, an' the tan hat an' coat. . . ."

"I can buy the rest," Dolores said absently.

If only, she prayed, she could get away before Peter came back.

She begged pad and pencil of Alma and wrote a note. It was the hardest thing she had ever done . . . she did not realize how little she had said, how incoherent it was. She leaned on the mission table and wrote, her tears blotting the words. Alma had left her alone and the tears would not be stayed.

"I'm going North, Peter. I opened Mr. Gaines' letter. Forgive me. . . . I'll go to see Judge Eldredge and get things straightened out. He must reconsider. It has all been such a useless deception. . . . I've been awfully happy . . . but it was all wrong and mistaken."

She opened the envelope which contained the fare money and divided it. In another covering the sealed half the money, Gaines' letter and her own.

When Farlowe and his wife arrived they found her very pale but completely controlled.

"I have had bad news,' 'she told them, as she had told Alma, "I must take the first train North. Will you give Mr. Comstock this when he returns? I can't reach him, I don't dare wait . . . he will understand."

"Couldn't you possibly wait until to-morrow?" Farlowe asked, in anxious astonishment. Hating herself for the lie, she shook her head and murmured something about illness.

As he took the letter from her Mrs. Farlowe said, troubled:

"But you can't travel that way, my dear."

"Alma has some of my things here. I can buy what I

need for the train. Would you . . . cash a check for me, Mr. Farlowe?"

She endorsed Asta's check and gave it to him, and he fished in his sagging pockets and put the bills into her hand.

"You're sure it's enough?" he laughed, genially. "I'm not afraid to have you draw on me. There's the camp for security and Mr. Comstock will be along presently."

"I have plenty," she assured him gratefully.

She was in a panic lest the Farlowes, on their return to the Inn, find Peter there and send him after her.

When they were leaving she found herself crying helplessly again. Mrs. Farlowe took her in her motherly arms and murmured over her. She looked over the bowed head to her husband. Surely something was seriously wrong? Illness? It must be the child's mother, or father.

After they had gone and Dolores had bathed her swollen eyes she went out and made her few purchases and got her accommodations. The trains were not crowded, she easily procured a lower berth to Washington.

She felt that she could not sit still and wait for the train to leave West Palm at three in the morning. She eventually crossed the bridge with Alma as her escort and boarded it at Palm Beach before midnight. When Alma had gone, promising to forward what remained of her belongings, when she sent an address, Dolores went straight to bed.

The train pulled out. It went across to West Palm and waited there. And there Kay Sterling boarded it, surrounded by laughing people. He went to his compartment and sat by the window smoking. Well, another season gone, he thought.

He also thought, briefly and uncomfortably, of Dolores. She had not needed to make that theatrical escape, nor to leave the torn frock of moonlight-and-lace. He recalled his alarm when he had eventually grown weary of waiting, and had gone to the upstairs room and found it empty.

A little fool—but a dear little fool. He would not have harmed her. After all she owed him something . . . for the chase she had led him . . . if only the fright of her life, the opening of her too-childish eyes . . . and the kiss he had stolen from her.

He wondered where she was. He had gone back to the houseboat several days later and found Asta packing to depart. Asta had been extremely uncommunicative.

And not very far away from him Dolores lay crying into her pillow. She was unhappy; she was ashamed; she was alone. She had nothing to companion her but her sense of failure and her resolution to give Peter what he wanted, even if, as it must, it broke her heart. . . .

CHAPTER XXI

DOLORES, going into the diner next morning, stopped in the narrow vestibule and drew back, her heart beating suffocatingly. Sterling faced her from the other end of the car. He was reading a newspaper, his honey colored head lowered. But she knew him immediately, and fled back to her unmade berth. She'd wait until he left the diner if she never had anything to eat again.

When she ventured out, he had gone and she was free to walk in and order her coffee and rolls.

She went without lunch, but healthy hunger forced her to dinner. He was not in the diner but she ate hurriedly, fearing that he would appear.

He did not see her until they had reached Washington. Then getting out of the car and hurrying down the platform she almost ran into him, but had turned and lost herself in the crowd before he was sufficiently recovered from his astonishment to follow her.

He found her in the waiting room, her little bag beside her.

"Dolores! Why did you run away?"

Did he mean now—or then . . . ?

She shook her head. Her eyes were dark pools of terror in her white face.

"Please . . . go away. . . . I don't want to talk to you."

He sat down beside her and smiled.

"You must. You owe me an explanation."

"No. . . ."

"My dear . . . I had no intention of harming you. . . . I merely was going to . . . scold you a little that night . . . and then take you back to the boat again. You can't forgive me?"

She shook her head. And then to his amazement, she nodded.

"Oh, I do forgive you," she told him, low. . . . "It was my fault. I was an imbecile."

"That's that then," he laughed. "Let us say . . . I was another. You are going to New York?"

She nodded.

"Alone?"

"Yes."

"And where have you been all these weeks? I have been away. I flew to Bimini, and had some fishing at Long Key. Then I came back and closed the house and caught a train . . . your train it seems."

She was silent. He said, coaxingly:

"You'll let me . . . ride back with you? It's not much of a trip you know . . . from here to New York."

After a long time during which her brain worked feverishly, she replied:

"Very well. . . ."

He looked at his watch and frowned.

"I must see a man here, on business. I have time to go to the Willard and back. Would you come with me?"

"I'd rather not."

He did not press her, keeping his astonished gaze from her inadequate clothes and luggage. He nodded and said:

"We'll meet on the train then. I have a good deal to say to you, Dolores."

When he had gone she rose and changed her ticket for a train that reach New York that night. Then she checked her bag and went out and lost herself in the Washington streets, her one idea being to escape from the cool blue eyes which had a trick of turning green, and from the touch of the compelling hand.

She would not return to the station until his train had gone.

She had something to eat at a tea-shop and came back

169

exhausted to board her train. She was safe, now. But, she thought for the first time, where should she go, when she reached New York? In a last emergency she must go to Asta. She had thought of nothing except that she must get away from Peter before he believed that she had trapped him, and beg Eldredge on her knees for Peter's freedom.

Sterling, coming to take his train, found himself faintly amused and stirred. If he knew anything about women that child was going through a bad time. It might be easy, now, to win her confidence. At any cost he was not going to let her escape from him again.

He went into the parlor-car to look for her. He had reserved the drawing room. She was not there and no one had seen her.

He went into the drawing room, angry and amazed. So she had tricked him again. The dim troubling of his blood became very definite under the compulsion of anger and the feeling that he had discovered her to be capable of evasion, stronger than he had ever imagined her. Well, she would come to New York and if he were not much mistaken by the next train. And he'd meet her. He'd find out where she was staying and what she meant to do.

The whole thing seemed absurdly like a comedy-melodrama to him. But he'd see it through. He might have been warned, he thought, by her unexpected surrender to his demands.

He remembered the torn gown and the mute message it had left for him. She had spirit, but if he were not badly mistaken she was frightened. Not so much of him as of something else. Well, he would find out what that was.

He reached New York, made his easy arrangements and proceeded to meet trains. He missed her in the crowd but caught her up as carrying her small bag herself she reached the pavement where the taxis stood. He touched her arm, laughing.

"You do make a habit of it, don't you?" he asked her softly.

She flung him one startled terrified glance, and ran, just the few steps to a waiting taxi which stood, the motor

170

going and the door open. He heard her gasp out an address in Gramercy Park.

When the taxi had pulled away he stood and fingered the clipped mustache thoughtfully. He knew now where she was going. It would not be hard to find her.

He turned and signalled his car.

In the taxi Dolores leaned back against the cushions. She was deathly white with hunger and fatigue and fear. She had given the driver Eldredge's address.

When she reached it she paid the driver and went up the steps of the apartment house. An elevator boy took her to the apartment—he was accustomed to directing all sorts of people to Judge Eldredge, at all hours. A maid caught the name she murmured and took her to a small reception room. She waited there, twisting one cold hand in the other.

Eldredge frowned when word reached him of her arrival. He spoke briefly to his pretty, serene-browed wife, and went from the room.

"Mrs. Comstock . . . ? Then he saw her face. "My *dear* child!" he said.

He took her to his library, put her into a deep chair and, ringing for the maid, gave orders.

"Don't try to talk. You look faint," he bade Dolores.

Presently he was urging her to drink a glass of sherry and nibble at some biscuits. Dolores obeyed and he noted that her teeth chattered against the rim of the glass.

"Now," he said, when she had finished. "How can I help you?"

She answered slowly, her color and her courage returning:

"I heard from Mr. Gaines that you had decided not to grant the annulment. I came to beg you to change your mind."

He shook his head, his eyes saddened.

"And if I do not . . . ?"

She put out her hands to him in a gesture of appeal.

"But you must! You see, Peter didn't understand. He thought that the papers had been signed. He came to Palm Beach to . . . to tell me so. . . . I knew he was wrong, I had had a wire from Mr. Gaines. Then when I found that

171

Mr. Gaines had written Peter fully I ran away to find you and beg you to reconsider."

"I don't understand," Eldredge told her. "Your husband came to Palm Beach? How long ago?"

She told him, flushing.

"But I am all at sea," Eldredge told her gently, "you must try and make me understand. Do you mean that you and your husband have been living together and that he thought I had granted the annulment, and that you knew I had not and let him think so?"

Her color deepened. She dropped her eyes and then raised them to his, leaning forward in her chair. She began to explain, rapidly, brokenly.

"In the beginning, don't you remember, we hadn't wanted to marry. Then I made him. I was frightened. I couldn't go on with it. I think he felt later that I had taken an unfair advantage, had forced him into the situation. But when we separated we knew we still loved each other. You knew it, too, Judge Eldredge. But we couldn't go back, on the old terms, we thought. I went down South . . . and things happened there . . . and I began to see all I had thrown away, and how much I needed him and wanted him, and what stupid, blind creatures we had been. Then he came down, looking for me . . . and I could see that he thought we were both free, and that he was willing to begin again on that basis. So I let him think so. He had talked to Mr. Gaines by telephone, long distance, and didn't understand. And I had had the wire. So I risked it. I went away with him, and we were happy. I thought we were so happy that when I had to tell him the truth he would realize, as I had, that our happiness hadn't come from his illusion of freedom, but from ourselves, from loving each other and growing to be comrades."

"I see," Eldredge said quietly.

"Then he went away on business. While he was gone a letter came from the lawyer to him. It had been waiting, weeks. It just said plainly that Mr. Gaines feared Peter hadn't understood him in their telephone conversation, and that he was following up a wire to me. It said that,

172

realizing how much Peter wanted his freedom, Mr. Gaines was ready to talk of other means. Divorce."

"What did you do then?"

"I was ashamed. I realized that he would know I had known all along, that he would think I had been laughing at him, making a fool of him. . . . I ran away. I took the first train back. I left the letter and a note for him. I told him I would implore you to set it right. It's the only way I can make it up to him."

"You believe that he won't come to see things the way you do now?"

"No. He'll hate me."

"What's to stop him," Eldredge asked, smiling, "from pretending he's free for the rest of your lives? My dear, doesn't it all seem a little strained and foolish to you, as if you were children playing hookey, children sowing your garden oats?"

"Then you won't annul it?" she asked him after a silence.

"No, I don't think you want me to. I don't think your Peter will want it when he understands. You can make him understand. Nothing stands in your way but a pride and a fear that he will be angry with you. Think how close you two have become on this holiday of yours! Can't you keep on, making holidays? Both of you were too young for marriage, for all that marriage entails, the adjustments and responsibilities, the uphill pull. But you were not too young for love. And you owe something, not only to each other, but to society. The institution may not be perfect—none is—but we have no substitutes. If you and Peter have found that you can be comrades and lovers you will find that you can be husband and wife. You have much to work toward. Marriage, I'll concede, isn't romance. It is home building, partnership, it is man and wife against the world. Man and wife . . . and children. Had you never thought of that?"

After a long time she put her folded arms on the desk and laid her head upon them. He waited, listening to her smothered sobbing and made no sound or gesture until she raised her distorted face and asked him, simply:

"What must I do?"

He leaned over, put a big clean handkerchief in her hand.

"You must wait. Peter will come to find you and you must have it out. You must face his anger at your deception. I don't think he will be angry long. He will have had time to think. And you must ask yourselves if you are strong enough to go on. If you have courage enough to make a real marriage of your love-experiment; if you have gallantry and belief in your love with which to create reality out of dreams, to build a marriage out of those toy bricks we call romance and passion and glamour. You must ask yourselves if you are worthy to have children. So few people are, my dear. You must question whether you are fit to share burdens, and artists enough to mould something enduring and beautiful from common human clay. It is easy to gratify the senses, Dolores, to give yourself just to Love, while Love lasts. But it is harder to give yourself to loving, which is not the same thing. There is no more difficult task on earth than the building of a house of life in which a man and woman may find permanent union."

She said, presently:

"We didn't look at it that way."

"Few people do until it's too late," he told her.

"I might write him," she said, "but . . . I couldn't put it on paper. When . . . when he gets over being angry, perhaps he'll come find me, as you said. I . . . I'm so ashamed, Judge Eldredge. . . . I've been so dishonest."

"You know," he reminded her, "that it couldn't last. He'd have to know, sooner or later. It was no kindness to him to let him live in his fool's paradise."

"Yes," she answered and then spoke, brokenly. "Yet we were so happy!" she mourned.

"It will all come right," he comforted her. "And now you will stay here to-night and get some rest, and then, if you'll let me advise you, you'll go home, to your people."

"My cousins?" she asked, mechanically. "But they don't know anything. They don't even know that we separated. They think I just left Peter for a holiday."

"No matter which way you and Peter decide," he said, "They'll have to know."

Later Mrs. Eldredge took her in charge and put her to bed in the pleasant guest room. She came out with shining eyes.

"Such a baby! Not much older than our own."

"Yes," Eldredge agreed, sighing, "that's the trouble."

He went to his library and sent a night letter to Peter at the address Dolores had given him. In effect the wire said . . . "When you reach New York . . . come straight to me."

Peter had been delayed in returning to the Point. He had found his man, outlined the scheme, the agent had telegraphed his principals and Peter had cooled his heels until a return message came, authorizing the agent to inspect the offered property and follow his own judgment. So Peter had finally brought the man back to camp with him, wanting to sing all the way, certain that success rode beside him.

At the Inn, Farlow's welcoming face was grave. Peter not noticing made the introductions, and asked hurriedly, happily, "Mrs. Comstock?"

He'd had a long drive. He was tired. But he wanted to see her at once, tell her his hunch had been justified.

"She went to New York," Farlowe told him.

"What!"

The inn-keeper gave him an envelope. Peter stepped aside, tore it open, read Dolores' note, thrusting the money automatically into his pocket. The agent, talking with Farlowe, cleared his throat impatiently. Peter looked at him blankly, and then, as if recognizing him, came toward the two men.

"I understand. Thanks," he told Farlowe, through wooden lips. "Well come along, Mr. Robbins, we'll look at the Point."

He arranged with Farlowe to accommodate Robbins and spent the short rest of the day tramping over the land. Robbins did not commit himself immediately. He must wire North in detail, fix the price. It would take time.

When Eldredge's message reached Peter he tore it up. Doubtless Dolores had seen the judge, and persuaded him

175

to alter his decision. Why should he see him? Gaines could make all arrangements.

He had read Gaines' letter hastily. The reference to a wire sent Dolores puzzled him, but he had other things to think about. The only conclusion he came to was that the telegram had not reached her before they went away together. Perhaps it had been waiting at the woman's house, with the letter.

In Dolores' note he could read nothing except that she knew they were still married, and that, by his reasoning, he had deceived her. So she had left him, angry, irreconcilable, to beg Eldredge to reconsider.

Oh, if he had told her himself, if he had urged his love and need of her as excuse, she might have understood! She did not deny that she'd been happy. Perhaps she would have forgiven him and gone on, knowing, as he had come to know, that there is no real freedom save the freedom of two who love.

He could not face her. He was too hurt, too bitterly disappointed, too enraged at himself for his cowardly evasion of the issue. If ever she wanted him, she could send for him. Meantime Eldredge had probably given in to her. How could anyone withstand—Dolores?

Robbins misunderstood his lack of interest in the projected sale. On the day he made his first cautious offers Peter did not seem to listen, he was frowning, looking out to sea. Sighing, the agent mentioned the top price which had been authorized by the men for whom he acted.

Peter took success calmly. Success was ashes when you couldn't share it, when no dear eyes looked their pride in you, and no beloved mouth kissed you for reward. Success, unshared, was pretty close to failure, thought Peter.

CHAPTER XXII

LATE spring had come to New England, not as it comes to the South with fevers and opulence, but sunny and cool, and gracious, as happy youth, softening the rugged contours with veils of rosy flowers, clothing the austere granite heart with drifts of green and shadows of mauve and blue.

Dolores getting off the train stood still a moment, surrounded by the familiar fragrance of the old town, a perfume compounded of sun and salt and lilac bloom, warm and virile and sweet.

She took a cab to her house. All the way there she sat with her hands clasped one within the other. What would they say? It was curious but now that she was here again homesickness took her, like a great wave. She had not felt homesick before, when she was far away, when miles of distance and leagues of experience and stretches of time lay between her and the quiet town.

She had said to Eldredge:

"I'm afraid to go back. . . ."

"We're always afraid to go back," he replied, "and few of us have the opportunity."

"But I must tell them something."

"Of course. Haven't you learned you can do nothing in this world without involving innocent people, somehow, somewhere?"

She had not thought of that before, she said.

She was coming back empty handed, even to material things. Most of her possessions were stored at Asta's in

177

town . . . well, she could send for those . . . and the things she had had with her in Palm Beach were at Alma's or in the tent on the Point. She closed her eyes in an agony of remembrance. The little brown tent with the door flap open to the wind and the sound of sea and rustling palms blowing through it. . . .

She had wired her cousins that she was arriving, but not the train. She could not endure to see them at the station. When she had dismissed the cab, and was walking up the path, she thought, her eyes on the square brick house and crowning deck, and the welcoming doorway . . . how strange that nothing is changed. The garden dreamed in the afternoon shadows, the peach blossoms drifted downwards, and the old swing creaked faintly in the light wind, a ghostly sound.

Before she could lift her hand to the knocker or touch the bell, the door opened. Cousin Carolyn, agitated and tremulous, stood there, Cousin Sarah, more controlled, beside her. They drew her in and spoke her name, tenderly.

"Dolores!"

Had she been away a year? Was she not coming back from a visit to Anna in Boston?

In the background Letty hovered, smiling. Martha would be in the kitchen, getting tea ready, Dolores thought. No, nothing had changed.

Her cousins drew her in, helped her with her things, set her bag aside.

"You'll want to make ready for tea," advised Cousin Carolyn briskly, her eyes bluer than ever behind her glasses.

"Your room," Cousin Sarah told her, "is in order . . . such a cleaning as we had. You gave us scant notice."

She spoke with the severe patience which Dolores remembered. And again it seemed as if no time had passed.

Her own room was the same. The immaculate white ruffles of the curtains blew in at the windows. The double row of trees outside were feathered with green. Upon the walls the marble bridges crossed the stream, the sentimental ladies and gentlemen wandered interminably

178

among the leaning willows, their romance still unfinished. Only the book shelves had a different look.

Her cousins left her and she bathed the dust from her face and hands, and brushed her dark hair until it gleamed like the purple black wings of a bird. Then she went down the stairs, her fingers lightly on the solid old banisters.

Her cousins were waiting in the drawing room. Miss Brewster sat in her teakwood chair, the footstool under her strapped slippers. The open sewing table stood beside her, with her embroidery, pale silks, gleaming needles, and worn old thimble. Sarah, grown plumper, sat nearby and viewed a perforated dress pattern which, Dolores thought, Mrs. Evans, the sewing woman, must have brought in that morning for her approval.

Tea was ready. As Cousin Carolyn poured her cup and handed it to Dolores she said, quietly:

"I am sorry to see that you have cut your hair. . . ."

Cousin Sarah nodded, laying the pattern aside and drawing closer to the table. Dolores said, rather faintly:

"Everyone does, you know. It needs cutting. But I was thinking of letting it grow."

While they drank their tea they asked her no questions. Instead they told her such news as had not reached her in their letters. This person had married; that one's father had died . . . and did she know that the eldest Lacy girl had lost her little boy? Such a pity, they said, resigned.

Once Cousin Sarah remarked:

"You are very tanned . . ." and Dolores nodded. Cousin Sarah added, absently: "I still have your great grandmother's cucumber-and-honey lotion recipe. It is said to be excellent for bleaching."

Not until Letty had taken away the tea things and Dolores had gone to the kitchen to speak to Martha, and had returned, did the cousins mention Peter.

Dolores was standing by the window, looking into the garden. Not far away the Spanish girl looked down at her from the wall, gay and beautiful, a little melancholy under her smiling, always the alien.

"When is Peter coming?" asked Cousin Carolyn, making a stitch in a rose petal.

Dolores turned from the window. She felt smothered, as if she could not breathe. She must tell them.

She said gently:

"He's not coming, Cousin Carolyn. I've left him."

There was a dead silence. The last sunshine slanted in, the swing creaked in the garden, tulips drooped in a silver vase. The lusters swung, flashing blue, and red, and purple in their crystal hearts.

"You've . . . left him?" repeated Cousin Carolyn, dully.

"Yes. . . ."

Cousin Sarah said, vigorously:

"I thought as much . . . when you wrote us you were going to Florida without him. Happy wives do not go away from their husbands, Dolores."

Dolores made no reply. Cousin Carolyn asked her, her voice dry as if her throat hurt her:

"*Why* have you left him?"

Dolores stared at her. . . . Why? Could she tell them . . . I have left him because I love him and because he must be free?

She came slowly across the room and sat down on the footstool. She looked up at the old, delicate face still bent over the embroidery and she marked how the thin, high veined hands shook, drawing the needle in and out. She sat, her arms folded on the elder woman's lap, and spoke, dimly:

"It wasn't his fault . . . we . . . didn't get on."

Cousin Sarah made a curious sound. She remarked:

"Well . . . if all the wives who 'didn't get on' left their husbands . . ." and left her sentence unfinished.

"Brewster women," Cousin Carolyn said with a sweet, aloof coldness, "have always been faithful to their vows. You took those vows, Dolores."

Her voice shook and trailed into silence.

Dolores said:

"I know. I'm ashamed. It . . . couldn't be. . . . I had to leave him."

Cousin Sarah sighed, heavily:

"We have reproached you very little, my dear, for your unconsidered step. We had not deserved such treatment. But we forgave you. We were always ready to welcome you and Peter home. And now you come and tell us you left him. Marriage," said Cousin Sarah, dreaming back across the years, "is not like a garment you can put on and take off, at will."

Cousin Carolyn nodded. A faint flush rose to her withered cheeks, and she asked, low:

"Tell us . . . we have a right to know . . . has . . . has Peter been unfaithful to you?"

"No, Cousin Carolyn."

Miss Brewster sat straighter in her chair. She asked, again:

"Has he been . . . unkind?"

"No . . . no. . . ."

Over her head which she bent now the sisters looked at one another. "A lovers' quarrel," said Miss Carolyn's relieved eyes, and Sarah nodded.

"You came straight here from Florida?"

"Yes. . . . I stayed in New York . . . a day or so . . . I wired you from there."

"Peter is in New York?"

"I don't know, Cousin Sarah. He . . . he was in Florida when I left."

"I see."

Cousin Carolyn asked, almost casually:

"What are you going to do now, Dolores?"

"I don't know." And she did not. Elredge had said definitely that he would not annul the marriage. But there must be other ways . . . if need be, she thought, shrinking, divorce.

After a time she said:

"Some arrangement must be made . . . I hadn't thought . . . not yet. I . . . I can't go back. . . ."

Over the faces of the sisters a shadow settled. Miss Carolyn's thin lips tightened. She almost whispered:

"You are not thinking of . . . divorcing Peter?"

She spoke the word as if it were unclean. Her very lips drew back from it.

181

"I don't know . . ." said Dolores dully, "if he wishes it. . . ."

Miss Carolyn said, sternly:

"There has never been a divorced woman in all our history. Women of our family do not soil themselves with such . . . expedients, Dolores."

Dolores sprang to her feet. Her face flamed and her eyes grew darker.

"What am I to do then?" she cried, thrusting her empty hands out to them, "what *can* I do?"

Miss Carolyn answered austerely:

"You can go back to your husband and keep your vows."

"No!"

She flung herself away from them and cast her slim body in the embrace of a wide-armed chair and wept stormily, shaken with tearing sobs.

The nervous tears rose to Miss Carolyn's eyes. She looked appealingly at her sister. Sarah rose and went from the room. When she returned she had something aromatic, faintly lavender, in a glass. She walked over to the huddled figure and touched her arm.

"Try and control yourself," she said, not ungently, "drink this—and make an effort at composure, Dolores."

Dolores shook her head. But Sarah with soft inescapable strength drew the girl's wet hands from her face and held the glass to her lips.

"There. We will say nothing further until you are more rested and more yourself," she said.

Miss Carolyn spoke:

"This is your home,' she told Dolores, measured, "Whatever you do or do not do, however little we approve, your home is here. Its doors are open to you. After we are gone it will belong to you, Dolores."

Dolores sat up and brushed childishly at her eyes with her clenched fist:

"I know," she said brokenly, "but I couldn't stay here, of course. I couldn't stay, I'd feel how unwanted I was . . . what a sacrifice you were making, having me. And what would I do? I wouldn't fit in any more. I never have,

182

really. I couldn't spend the rest of my life . . . just . . . dusting and gardening and playing the piano and growing old. . . . I couldn't!"

Carolyn asked, quietly:

"Where else could you go?"

"I don't know. . . . I could find work . . . a place to live . . . somewhere where people didn't know me," Dolores answered dully.

Work? It was a foreign word to Miss Carolyn's ears. She said, dryly:

"Now you are being childish, Dolores. You belong here. If you leave your husband you must stay. Surely that is understood. And . . ." she added, gently, "you are all we have, Sarah and I. . . ."

"I know," answered Dolores, staring straight ahead of her, "I . . . I've treated you both abominably. I haven't any excuse. I . . . didn't think."

"No, you didn't think," Sarah agreed. "Young people rarely do."

After a moment Carolyn said, briskly:

"Go to your room, Dolores, and lie down. You need rest. Letty will bring your supper up. To-morrow things may look quite differently to you. We will be able to talk over your problem, fully. But you must give us more of your confidence, my dear, than you have done, so far."

She rose and went to the girl, putting her spare arm about her, raising her to her feet. She and Sarah went up the stairs, Dolores between them. No one spoke. They left her, there in the quiet bedroom, with the wind blowing and the faded colors of the wall paper dim in the approaching twilight. They kissed her and one of them said:

"We are glad you have come. . . ."

Then they left her and went downstairs and sat, one with her embroidery, and the other with her patterns, two confused elderly women, heartsick and frightened, utterly bewildered, holding hard to their standards of gentleness and courtesy, of courage and silence in the face of disaster.

Dolores lay face down on the bed. She stretched out her arms to the cool linen, the white pillows. She was back

183

once more in the cage, a prisoner of the tradition she had broken, captive of an inexorable kindness. She saw herself living on in the old house, growing older, her blood cooling, her step losing its elasticity. She saw the round of days, serene and monotonous. She saw the gallantry with which her cousins would face curiosity and questions, with which they would repell the inquistive. Gossip would fling itself in vain against the solid walls of the old house. She saw herself fading, she saw herself . . . alone.

"No . . . no . . . no . . ." she whispered.

Peter. She mustn't think of Peter. She mustn't think of marriage as Eldredge had made her see it. Sh must think of nothing except that Peter must be unhampered, able to live his own life.

The shadows thickened in the room, the ladies and gentlemen in the faded painted groves were unrecognizable now. Downstairs the two elderly women sat talking quietly, until Letty came in to light the lamps.

CHAPTER XXIII

THE days passed draggingly, and were like nightmares dreamed in a familiar setting in which beauty wore the countenance of peace. The spring sun shone, the birds sang, the trees were leafed in tenderest green, the garden was gay with color and narcotic with scent. But she seemed to herself like a figure in an endless play, moving through the old rooms, sitting with her cousins, seeing occasional visitors, and evading their kindly and unsuspecting questions about Peter. Every day there was the same quiet clash of wills, the same voices, well bred, gentle, asking the same questions: "Why have you left Peter?" "Why do you not give us your confidence?" "We do not find your reasons adult or adequate."

She wrote to Judge Eldredge as she had promised. "I have told them," she said, in part; "they do not understand. I don't know what will become of us unless you help us."

But she knew that he would not.

He replied that he had not heard from Peter; that he had had a caller, a Mr. Sterling, who had asked him for her address. He had not given it, not knowing her wishes.

She wrote back, frantically, "no one must know where I am."

She wondered how Sterling had traced her. But it had not been very difficult, as he heard the address given the taxi driver at the station and went there and made guarded inquiries of doorman and elevator boy. But from Eldredge himself he received no information.

Toward the first of June Miss Carolyn was called to the telephone. She listened, and then hanging up the receiver went out to look for Dolores. She found her in the garden in the swing, idle, a closed book in her lap, the sunlight on her empty hands and her still, rebellious face. Miss Carolyn stood beside the old green structure, her hand upon the supports.

"Dolores, I've had bad news."

The book fell to the floor of the swing. Dolores sat upright, her face a mask of fear.

"Peter?"

If Miss Carolyn's heart beat faster at that betrayal she said nothing. She answered instead:

"No, Peter's father. He is very ill. They have telephoned. They are unable to find Peter. It is known that you are here, of course, so the doctor and housekeeper have sent word, asking you to go to Mr. Comstock and to get in touch with Peter."

Dolores said, breathlessly:

"But I can't go . . . how can I?"

Miss Carolyn asked sternly:

"How can you not? Has Peter been on bad terms with his father since your marriage?"

"Yes. Mr. Comstock wanted us to come home."

"It is your duty to get word to your husband; your duty to go to his father."

"But . . ."

Miss Carolyn looked at her impatiently:

"There can be no argument, my dear."

"Oh, but Cousin Carolyn . . . with the situation between Peter and me as it is . . ."

"You shall go to Mr. Comstock at once," said Cousin Carolyn implacably. "You owe me some obedience! You must find his Peter for him, you must bring him some comfort, some human affection. First of all you must telegraph Peter at every possible or probably address."

After a minute Dolores nodded, slowly. She rose and made ready for the street. Miss Carolyn communicated

186

with the Comstock house, telling the nurse that Mr. Comstock's daughter-in-law would reach there shortly. Meantime she would wire her husband.

Dolores packed a small bag and went to the telegraph office. She wired to the Point, although she had very little hope of its reaching him; she wired Hodge Meadows, and, after a search in a New York telephone book, Laff Maynard. Then she hired a car to take her to the mill town.

All the way she was in an agony of nervousness. What would she say to this sick old man? She scarcely knew him, had seen him only a scant dozen times since her childhood. Peter's father . . . who had wronged Peter so bitterly. She knew that she must keep from him any suggestion of trouble between Peter and herself.

Reaching the gloomy house in which the blinds were drawn against the benevolence of the sun, she found herself shuddering. How could Peter have lived there . . . enduring the oppressive atmosphere which seemed to go out from the place like a slow, gray fog? How could she bear to stay there . . . even for a moment?

But she went in. The agitated housekeeper met her in the doorway, her hands outstretched. She had been with Mr. Comstock since his second marriage.

Dolores knew her by name. She took the hands, made an effort at smiling.

"It's Mrs. Luce?"

Mrs. Luce's face worked. Her sunken eyes streamed with tears.

"Oh, thank God you've come!" she said. "Have you found Mr. Peter for us?"

"He's . . . travelling," Dolores said. "I've wired. He'll come, Mrs. Luce, don't worry."

"His father wants him," said the woman simply. "He's been fretting for him a year. But he's obstinate. He wouldn't send or beg him to come home." She paused and added quaintly, "Mrs. Peter . . ." and the quick tears came to Dolores' eyes.

"Are you sure," she asked timidly, "that he'll see me . . . ?"

Mrs. Luce nodded.

187

"We haven't said anything but . . . but here comes the doctor."

Doctor Hatton, a heavy, middle-aged man with a controlled, sagacious face, came down the long stairs. He looked from Dolores to Mrs. Luce in inquiry.

Mrs. Luce explained.

"Peter's wife?" He had brought Peter into the world, "and where's the boy?"

Dolores repeated:

"He . . . has been travelling in Florida on business. I've wired to all the places where he would be likely to stop."

Hatton looked at her shrewdly. It was evident, to him, that she herself had not been in touch with her husband lately. He shrugged, sighing . . . these young people. However, it was not his business. His business was the sick man upstairs.

"I'm glad you've come. Mr. Comstock needs someone of his own about him."

"What . . . was it?"

"Stroke. He is better now. He can move, and speak. But he must be kept quiet. We have a long siege ahead of us. You'll help."

Later, Mrs. Luce took her to a plain, gloomy room with massive furniture and chocolate brown walls, "Peter's," she told her, smiling a little.

Dolores, when Mrs. Luce had left her, looked about her. Here he had lived, slept, dreamed; from this room he had escaped to her.

The drab ugliness of the place took on the beauty of associated things. She touched the great bed, with a gentle hand, looked at the scarred desk, smiled faintly at her distorted reflection in the dim mirror which had for so many years given back his face.

Looking at the room, standing there, only her eyes moving, she understood Peter better than she had ever understood him.

Presently the nurse came and knocked.

"Mrs. Comstock? We have told him, he is asking for you."

188

Her heart beating thickly with nervousness, she followed the silent stepping woman to another door. The nurse opened it and stood aside to let her enter. Crossing the threshold of the darkened room with its smell of medicine and illness was one of the hardest things she had ever done.

Ashabel Comstock lay in a tremendous bed, the pillows no whiter than his gaunt face. Under the bedclothes his emaciated figure seemed preternaturally long. He lifted a shaking hand upon which the flesh was taut over the big bones.

"Peter's . . . wife?" he murmured in a dry, rattling voice. She nodded, trying to control the shaking of her lips. He turned his head with infinite slowness and motioned toward the straight backed chair beside the bed.

"Sit down," he ordered slowly.

His eyes were very gray, they were like Peter's. They burned with a smouldering unextinguished fire under his heavy brows. He folded his hands across his lean breast and looked at her so long and searchingly that she thought she must scream if the regard endured another moment.

"Young," he said, with that dry difficulty. "Pretty." He was silent, and then said suddenly, "The beauty of the flesh is but a snare."

The nurse had gone. Dolores sat, stiffly erect, alone, terribly frightened, with the sick wandering old man.

He closed his eyes for a long minute. Then he opened them and asked:

"Peter?"

She leaned nearer, conquering the repulsion of youth and health for sickness and old age. She said, gently, clearly:

"He is coming. . . ."

A gleam of satisfaction, like wintry sunshine, passed over the old face. Presently, he did not speak again, and she saw that he slept. She was afraid to move and sat there, alone with his heavy breathing, and the shadows of the terrifying room, until the nurse came in to release her.

Moving through the old house during the long following hours, eating mechanically what was set before her, she lived the slow, leaden days. Every day her father-in-law sent for her. Sometimes he would speak. And sometimes he would say nothing, only his restless hands moving. And slowly, he grew a little stronger.

When she had been there three days he asked her suddenly:

"You are happy . . . you and Peter?"

Happy! She had a wild desire to laugh, to cry. She controlled the rising hysteria and answered wondering why it was that you must always lie to spare someone:

"Very happy."

Comstock nodded.

"He is a good boy. I have been wrong. I tried to force him to my paths. I tried to play God. I blasphemed. I was old when he was born. I was impatient." His pitiful voice slurred and stopped, then he said suddenly, strongly, "But he was rebellious. He owed me duty and gave it not. If he had come home . . . When is he coming, Daughter?"

Her heart turned over at the little word. She said, without hope:

"Soon. He is on his way."

Another time he spoke to her of his dead wife, Peter's mother.

"Young, as you are. Beautiful. In the drawer there, in the stand, the photograph."

She understood and fetched it for him. He held it in his hands and looked at it without speaking. Then:

"Her son. I failed her. I . . . she comes to me, she reproaches me . . . she asks me, crying in that quiet way she had . . . 'Where is my boy, Ashabel, what have you done with him?' "

After a while he motioned her to put the picture under his pillow. When she had done so, pitifully, he said:

"I drove him away. I was angry at him. He had affronted all that was most sacred to me. I set myself up to judge him, greater than God."

After a silence he asked her:

"When will he come back?"

"Soon . . ." she said, as she had said every day.

He nodded, satisfied for the moment.

"I shall not ask him to stay," he said with an effort, "but I must see him again . . . tell him . . . I was mistaken . . . I have an accounting to make . . . Ellie. . . ."

After a time he murmured, so low she had to bend down to hear the words:

"He was so young and I so old."

For the first time she put her warm, ivory smooth hand on his and saw the miracle of his difficult smile. He closed his bony fingers about it, death clinging to life, and sighed as if the swift current of her blood, the warm virility of her flesh had penetrated his dryness and coldness, his deathlike inertia.

"Daughter . . ."

He slept again, his hand enclosing hers. She sat there and felt her fingers grow numb. Her heart ached with pity. There had been so much love here, in this tenacious heart, and Peter had never known: Love enough to bridge the gap between them, to make for eventual understanding. And Peter might never know. God, she prayed suddenly, send Peter home to his father. . . .

He grew so that he wanted her with him most of the time. She was constantly in the sickroom, whether he waked or slept, a glowing, pale flower budding from the darkness. The doctor and nurse conferred, nodded with satisfaction.

"You do him good, Mrs. Comstock. Soon, we'll have him out of the woods. With care, he will live years. If only that boy would come home!"

She thought:

"Will he never come?"

He was coming. He had left Florida. He stayed, with the Point which no longer belonged to him, as his headquarters, enduring the hot days and long nights, trying to work out his problem. His thoughts swung around one axis only. He and Dolores were man and wife. They were not free. He thought, we never shall be, no matter what any court may say. We are bound, always. There must be, he thought, some way in which he might reach her and make her see. But she did not wish to see. She had left him. She had to make a holiday of love. . . .

When the wire came, signed by Dolores with the doctor's name, he packed and took the first train. This was a summons he could not ignore. When he reached New York, so engrossed in his thoughts that he forgot to wonder how old Hatton had learned his address, he found that there was a lapse of some hours before he could get a train home. He remembered Eldredge's wire. He hesitated, wondering what he could have to say to him. He would not go. No, he would go and see. If Dolores desired freedom, she should have it.

CHAPTER XXIV

AFTER some difficulty he found Eldredge at his home. He said, standing rather defiantly erect:

"I've had word that my father is very ill. I am on my way home. But first, I came to you, sir."

"Why didn't you come before?"

Peter said nothing. Eldredge gestured to a chair.

"How long have you?"

Peter told him; the Judge nodded.

"Time enough. Your wife has been here. I wired you when she left me. She was extremely upset to find that I would not sign the papers which would give you what you are pleased to call your freedom."

"I know."

Eldredge asked, regarding him steadily:

"I suppose you know she loves you."

Peter looked him straight in the eyes. He answered slowly:

"It's not enough, sir."

Eldredge lifted his head.

"So you've learned that?" he commented.

Peter told him, heavily:

"We were a couple of young fools. I, the more foolish of the two. I thought we could build a new world, that love and loyalty would be more likely to endure if you didn't bind them."

Eldredge smiled at him.

"And what do you think now?"

"What am I to think?" asked Peter desperately. "I can't seem to detach myself. It isn't just A Problem. It's *our* problem. When we ran away this last time I knew we were married—and I let her think that we were not. . . ."

Eldredge exclaimed in amazement and Peter looked at him:

"What did you say, sir?"

"*You* knew?"

"Why yes," Peter answered puzzled. "I talked to Gaines over the telephone before I went South. The connection was poor—but he made it clear enough. . . ."

"And you let her believe . . . ?"

"Oh, I don't make any excuse for myself! When I saw that she thought I had come down to give her her freedom, and believed we were back where we started, with a clear road ahead, I kept silent."

"Dolores knew too," Eldredge told him, bluntly. "Gaines had wired her."

Peter stared at him wildly.

"Then . . . then . . . ?"

"Oh, think it out for yourself . . . you were at cross purposes. Each of you thought he was deceiving the other. Each of you thought that to the other the freedom, the adventure—the illegality—mattered. So when Dolores saw that letter to you from your lawyer and jumped to the conclusion that you would hate her for her deception, she came back to beg me to give you your freedom. She doesn't want hers, Peter. But she thinks you want yours. And she's learned to love you enough to believe that her own heartbreak doesn't matter."

Peter's eyes were shining, then; suddenly, they were dim.

"She was thinking . . . about *me*, when she left?" he asked slowly.

"Yes. . . ."

"Can you tell me where she is?"

"No. But you'll find out. I gave my word I would not tell you. But I didn't promise I wouldn't see you."

"I must see my father," Peter said after a pause. "We . . . he was an elderly man when I was born. You under-

194

stand that, sir? We never understood each other very well. He was stern, undemonstrative. He hated my wanting to write. He destroyed my manuscripts . . . he told me they were evil, sacrilegious. He was wrong. They were just . . . awfully young. . . . I was trying to overturn the world, and the old institutions, and I had nothing to offer in their place. I didn't know that then, but I've had plenty of time to think since."

"You'll go on with your writing?"

"No. At least, not now. I'm going back home and see what my father wants of me. I've thought of going. Wanted to go many times, but something held me back."

Eldredge rose.

"Go then. I won't keep you. You might miss your train. You'll work things out. You're growing up."

"And Dolores . . . ?"

Eldredge shook his head.

"I can't advise you. But you'll find the way. I told her . . ." and here he smiled, charmingly, "I told her I washed my hands of you both. I made her understand that the proposed annulment was out of the question in the circumstances. The rest, the solution, lies between you two. That's marriage, you know: two people, working things out, together."

He held out his hand and Peter took it.

"Thank you. . . ."

Later, on the train, he sat as the hours went by, deep in his chaotic thoughts. Only one thing was clear. When he had seen his father he must find Dolores. He must give her what she wanted. If Eldredge were mistaken . . . and he prayed that he might not be . . . and Dolores wished her freedom there must be a way to give it to her. She was his responsibility, her happiness was in his care. He had wronged her deeply, as he now saw it. He had colored her mind with his immature dreams, and had blamed their failure upon her. But their failure did not lie at her doorstep, nor at his. These dreams had never been real enough to fail. They had been the green fruit of inexperience, the maunderings of a mind nourished on books and trumpet-

195

sounding words that held in them nothing of the verities of life, and living.

But she had been his wife. She was that still. They had played at marriage. They had played at love. Now the playtime was over and they must face the fact that they had done something from which they would never escape, which had left its mark on them both, which they could never undo or forget even if they went their separate ways.

He must find her and ask her to forgive him.

He had wired Dr. Hatton that he was coming, but had not named the train, wiring as he did from Florida. So no one met him at the smoke-stained, familiar station. It was evening when he reached his own door and, walking up the steps with a sense of unreality, put his hand to the bell. The door opened. Dolores stood there, very pale and calm. She said, as he stared at her, uncomprehending:

"I'm glad you've come, Peter."

He was dimly aware of Mrs. Luce, crying, in the background, of Hatton hurrying out of the long drawing room, of a white uniformed figure on the stairs. Someone took his bag. They were watching, all of them.

Like a man in a dream he forced himself into the conventional motions of life. He came forward, took her cold hands in his own, kissed her cheek, asked: "How is he . . . ?"

Hatton had his hand now, as he turned:

"Wretched boy . . . we've been frantic trying to find you. . . "

"The wire to the Point was delayed," he answered mechanically, "I was away for a day or so."

Hatton hurried him up the stairs.

"He is better," he told him. "We have to go slow, of course."

At the door he found himself alone with Dolores for a scant moment. She whispered, her hand on his:

"I've told your father nothing. You understand?"

He nodded. Dolores stepped back, and he went in alone.

He stood there awkwardly by the big bed, looking down. His father lifted a hand and Peter took it in his own. Ashabel Comstock said, weakly, smiling a little:

"She told us you would come."

Suddenly Peter felt himself on his knees, his head bent on the counterpane. The hard old hand touched his hair a moment. Comstock murmured:

"I wanted to ask you . . . I may not have much time . . . I wanted to say . . . forgive me. I had no right to interfere with your life, my boy, no matter how mistaken I thought you. It was a phase. It would not have lasted long. You were bound to come back to the right path, the only way . . . Ellie's son."

Peter said, sobbing:

"Father. . . ."

The old man murmured, astonished and wistful:

"Tears . . . ?"

He felt them on his hands, life giving. He touched the bent head again. He said:

"If God spares me . . ."

Half an hour later Peter came out of the sickroom. The nurse and Hatton came from the room opposite, where they had been sitting, waiting, the door open. Peter said, making no attempt to conceal his disturbance:

"He's asleep now. I hope . . . I hope I haven't upset him, Doctor Hatton?"

"It's the upset he needed," answered the doctor cheerfully. "Don't look so, Peter. He's all right. He has turned the corner. You're our best medicine, you and that wife of yours."

"Where is she?"

"Downstairs, with Mrs. Luce, seeing that the fatted calf is killed."

"Stay with us," begged Peter, suddenly terribly shy, "I haven't seen you for so long."

"No, you were always too healthy," chuckled Hatton pleasantly.

The nurse and Hatton, Peter and Dolores had their late supper in the panelled, dark room. But there were flowers on the table and a good deal of laughter and more talk. Peter told, a little proudly, about his sale of the Point. Dolores listened quietly. She was supposed to know all this, she thought.

When Hatton had gone on to his other patients and the nurse was busy with the sick man, Peter and Dolores sat alone in the library, and for a moment neither spoke. Then Peter said:

"I have seen Judge Eldredge."

She did not answer.

"He did not tell me where you were . . . he said . . . I should find you. Dolores . . . *have* I found you?"

"I don't know, Peter," she whispered.

"Nor I." After a pause he added in a curiously conventional tone: "It was good of you to come to my father. How did you know?"

She explained, carefully:

"I was at home. . . . Cousin Carolyn made me come. . . . Mrs. Luce telephoned her. She knew I was back . . . and they couldn't find you."

"I see. You must have hated coming."

"At first. Then I was glad. Peter, he loves you very much."

"Yes," said Peter gravely.

"You'll stay with him?" she begged.

"As long as he needs me. . . ."

"And then?"

He did not answer for a moment. Then he said:

"I'm going back to the mills, to-morrow. I've told him. I think I can make good there. When he is well . . . he won't be strong enough to take it all on his own shoulders. I want to learn from the beginning. I want to carry on."

She leaned forward in the big chair, her eyes intent upon his:

"You will loathe it!"

"Perhaps so." He laughed suddenly. "What does that matter? I'll learn not to. It must have something in it, to have shaped men's lives as it has done. I want to find out what that thing is. . . ."

After a moment she said:

"And the writing? You said you'd never write again. Did you mean it?"

He looked at her as if astonished at her wisdom.

"Of course I didn't mean it. I shall write again. But not

198

now; not until I have something to write about. You see, Dolores, I've found out that I know very little."

"Peter," she said presently, making a palpable effort, "we have to talk about ourselves. I had to tell Cousin Carolyn and Cousin Sarah something. I said I'd left you."

"What did they say?" he asked, frowning.

"They were hurt . . . terribly. They don't understand. There's no way of making them understand."

"I know. It must have been difficult for you, and for them, Dolores. Can't we talk . . . unemotionally. Can't we thrash things out . . . we never have, you know; not that first time in New York, nor when I came to Florida. Isn't it time now?"

She said, very low:

"Yes. . . ."

"What is it you want?" he asked her, looking at her still, pale face, the lashes drooped veiling the dark eyes. "What have I done to you—what have we done to each other? Begin at the beginning, Dolores . . . as if I were . . ." he smiled and concluded with a curious, deep meaning . . . "a stranger."

She lifted her eyes then and folded her hands, one within the other. That strange quality she had of stillness, of power held in leash seemed to emanate from her. She sat immobile, only her eyes moved and her lips. She spoke slowly, almost painfully:

"We were children," she told him. "I was a child in a garden, and you were a child in a big, shadowy house. And we loved each other . . . as children love. Then you escaped, as you thought, from the great house and the lack of understanding, and all the things that irked you, and went out . . . into what you thought was the world. And there you dreamed that nothing mattered but the freedom of the individual, and that you were chosen to preach this gospel, and set what was wrong and wicked and sordid in the world to rights. They were fine dreams. And you shared them with me, until I caught fire. I was a child reading fairy tales. The old beliefs, the old standards, the old faiths, you thought sick toothless dragons, which still held the power to threaten people, and make them unhappy. So you were a knight with a bright new lance riding to destroy these dragons forever. . . ."

She paused, and he held his breath. There was something so uncanny about her still beauty and her low voice, speaking dreamily. Over in a dark corner a great clock ticked out the minutes. The heavy draperies swung at long windows to a night wind. They heard the footsteps of Mrs. Luce on the stairs, and the sickroom door opened and closed.

"Go on, Dolores. . . ."

"I shared your dreams," she repeated, "and then, when the trouble came to you here, when you and your father forgot—if you had ever known it—that there was love between you, and saw only misunderstanding and hate, you came to me when I was waiting in the garden. And the fairytale held. If you were going out into life to fight your ancient dragons, I must go too. I `.` . . I was young and alive and vital, and I was imprisoned in tradition and peace."

"Dear . . ." he said.

But she lifted her hand and stopped him.

"So we went together. We were to be a shining example. We would defy that dragon, marriage . . . the superstition that fettered people to the same rock, galling them with chains, crushing their separate personalities. So we went, and at the first test I was afraid. I . . . I was two people then. I was Dolores, in a fairytale, and I was Dolores, terribly young and frightened, with all my people calling out in my blood, with the shadow of my house, and the men who had built it, and the women who had lived in it, lying across my heart. So I told you I couldn't go on and we went away and stood up before a man and said the words he asked us to say and . . . were married."

She was silent. They were far away, both of them, back in Port Chester . . . in the spring.

"We belonged to each other then," she said simply, "and it was all a wonder. Passion. Loving. Meeting each other's desire. And not knowing that there was more than that. Not caring. Not being able when the time came to face the petty things . . . work and worry and jealousy, nd adjustment. And so, we ran away again. We said—it's not too late to strike off the chains. As lightly as we had taken our vows we forgot them, Peter."

"Dolores . . ."

"Ah, don't speak now. Let me finish. I've had time enough to know what I must say. We ran away, Peter, not from each other, as we thought, but from consequences, from responsibilities, from living, from truth."

"I came back to you," he said softly.

"What drove you?" she asked him deeply.

He said nothing for a moment. Then answered, simply: "I wanted you."

She said, low, a slow flush rising under the ivory of her pallor:

"You wanted my hands and my lips and my body; as I wanted yours. And we pretended that we could appease our gods and be true to our dreams if we took each other in a make believe freedom."

"Ah, Dolores . . ."

"So once more," she said, "we ran from life, into our dream world, laughter and loving. How long would that have lasted, Peter? It had no roots. It was all wonder and desire—it was escape. And I lied to you by keeping silent. You've seen Judge Eldredge, he must have told you that I knew all along that we were still married. I thought . . . 'd risk it. I wanted you so much."

"I know, too," said Peter. "I knew the night I found you. But I thought what you thought. So I kept silent, too."

For a moment they looked at each other. There was laughter in their hearts, and tears.

"Such silly children," Dolores said presently, "you and making believe, when a word might have set it clear. But was afraid of that word."

"And I too," he said.

"Then," she went on, "when I saw Gaines' letter to you and knew how soon you would find out . . . I couldn't face you, I was too ashamed. I'd let you live in a dream, thought, I'd let you believe a mockery. You would despise me for it. I wasn't strong enough to say all we ever believed is mirage too. I thought that when you learned

201

that we were still man and wife, the old rebellions would seize you, and you'd feel that we'd quarrel and misunderstand. I thought you'd feel yourself trapped by circumstance again and would want me no longer. That the glamour would go, as it had once gone. And so, rather than tell you, I left you."

"And what do you think now?" he asked her.

"Now," she answered steadily, "I know that glamour must go, sooner or later, married or unmarried. But I no longer want it, except as a means to an end. For in marriage or out of marriage it is not enough."

He made a movement as if he would go to her and then sat back again in his chair. The one lamp that burned cast a circle of yellow light. Footsteps passed, echoing, on the street below. Someone spoke beyond the windows, they heard the voice, but not the trivial words.

"What *do* you want, Dolores?"

She lifted her lovely, steady eyes to his own.

"Everything!"

"Everything?"

"All we have shirked, and set aside! Trouble, and sharing, and hope, and the old gods, the old standards. Going on, working, helping, failing perhaps, but never defeated. I'm done with defeat."

He asked, hushed:

"Where did you learn this, Dolores?"

She smiled for the first time and he held his breath at the wonder of it.

"I've always known it. All women do. They are born knowing. It's just that—I forgot. I began to remember, there, on the Point. I remembered more when I left you, when I sat with Judge Eldredge that night in his library, and listened to what he had to say. I remembered, after I came home, back to the garden. And since I have been here, here in your house, Peter, sitting beside your father I have remembered the rest. I'll never forget now. If I can't have everything, Peter, I want nothing. Half measures won't do, any more."

He said:

"There'll be times when it will be hard, Dolores. . . ."

202

"I know. It's because we thought it would be so easy that we failed."

After a pause he told her:

"If only you'd waited. I was beginning to remember too. If we had been together when the letter came I would have taken you in my arms and told you, and asked for forgiveness and another chance."

"Would you, Peter?"

She said nothing. After a time he said, simply:

"We love each other. . . ."

"Yes, Peter."

"Is it enough to go on?"

For the first time she faltered, moving uneasily in her chair.

"If . . . if . . ."

He rose and went to her and knelt down beside her, and laid his arm lightly about her waist.

"If what?"

"If we are worthy of it . . ." she breathed.

He asked her, low:

"Can we not become so? Dolores . . . shall we build a marriage out of the love that is between us? Will you let me take you into my heart and life and arms forever? Will you help me, where I fail?"

"It's so big . . ." she told him.

"Yes. . . ."

After a time he said, looking up at her:

"I want you as I've never had you. As my wife. . . ."

"I'm ready," she said.

Then he asked her, for the third time in their tangled destinies:

"You won't be afraid . . . or sorry?"

"Sometimes I'll be afraid," she answered, "but I'll never be sorry. . . ."

"After all," he said, "we've won something out of all the misunderstanding and the deception, and the cross-purposes. We've won through to honesty. There won't be any barriers now. That's something this generation has learned, at all events; it's learned to drag out all the secret dark things and fling them down in the sunlight of sanity. Better

203

that, better the exposure of all the frailties and distortions and deformities than to let things fester in silence and terror."

He knelt, straightly, drew her head against his breast, bent his mouth to hers. The kiss was a sacrament, and a promise. The kiss was the wine of courage.

After a long time, she whispered:

"That was—marrying." And then she added, entreatingly, "Will you say the words, with me?"

He understood, nodded, his cheek against the soft darkness of her hair. They spoke in beautiful broken sentences, so low that only their hearts heard clearly:

"I take thee, Peter. . . ."

"I take thee, Dolores. . . ."

And then, clearer:

"For better, for worse, in sickness and in health . . . till death do us part. . . ."

Then they were silent, thinking of their vows.

CHAPTER XXV

THEY were sitting side by side on the old Empire couch when the nurse came in.

"Mr. Comstock is asking for you both," she said, hesitating.

Peter jumped to his feet.

"Is he—worse?"

"No . . ." said the nurse hurriedly, "no . . . he's been asleep. He just woke and had some hot milk . . . he will sleep again now. But he wanted to see you . . . to say good-night."

"We'll come up," said Peter.

They followed her, hand in hand, up the stairs. Peter said, pausing:

"I didn't ask you . . . some day we'll have our own house. But now . . . he's sick . . . and old. Would you be willing to live here, Dolores? It's such a gloomy old barn . . . and you'd be alone all day. . . ."

"I'll love it," she said instantly. "We'll open the shutters and let the sunlight in. It won't be gloomy, Peter, any more. You'll see. And I won't be alone . . . always," she said, bravely.

He took her to his heart, there on the stairs, and kissed her. From the landing the nurse saw them, and drew back waiting, smiling a little, tolerantly, wisely. Young things . . young things!

She had to wait a long minute. They stood there, perilously poised on the narrow treads, listening to each other's o be alone always? Children in this great house, children's laughter, children's footsteps, the prints of stubby fingers on the old walls: Sunshine in the windows, the day's work, the night's rest: Life ahead of them, beckoning them on.

Presently they joined the patient woman and she opened the door of their father's room, and they went in and stood hand in hand beside the bed where he lay. There was a little color on the gaunt cheeks, he lay quite high upon the pillows and smiled at them.

"You'll stay with me?"

"Yes, father."

He nodded, deeply content.

"It's yours now," he murmured, "the house . . . everything. I'm an old man. . . ."

Peter said clearly:

"You're going to be well soon. We have so much to talk about when you're stronger. The business. . . ."

Ashabel Comstock turned his head and looked at Dolores, smiling:

"He's going back to the mills," he told her, as if in confidence.

"I know," she said, "I'm glad."

A gleam of frosty humor passed over the old face.

"What he'll do to them!" he sighed.

Then he was silent and they thought he slept and tiptoed from the room again. But he did not sleep. He watched them go under half closed lids, and his eyes held a difficult, unaccustomed tenderness. He saw the old house as Dolores had seen it, sunlit and echoing to the high voices of his children's children. He would die, one day, but his race would go on, and his untarnished name. And when he died he could make his peace with Ellie.

Mrs. Luce passed Peter and Dolores in the hall and said good-night, smiling cheerfully for the first time in days.

"It's good to have you home again," she said.

Dolores laid her hand on the latch of Peter's own door.

"They've put us in here," she said.

It was very late. The town was quiet, it slept under a

soft June sky. Peter moved about the room with idle fingers.

"Funny old place," he murmured, "somehow it's fine to be back."

Dolores nodded. After a time, tall and slender in her nightgown she stood by the window and motioned to him to join her. Together they looked out over the drowsy streets and listened to the rustle of the trees and the voice, far away, of a river singing in its sleep.

He said, dreamily:

"Home. . . ."

Dolores leaned back against his hard young arm. She answered, seeing more deeply than he saw, wiser than he, with woman's incredible wisdom:

"We'll make it so. . . ."

They saw a star hanging tremulous above the branches of the highest trees, a star that burned from silver to scarlet, a star that laughed at them and was their friend.

He cried out, eager, triumphant:

"There's so much to be done . . . so much waiting for us."

She nodded and said:

"If you've time . . . we'll go see Cousin Carolyn and Cousin Sarah . . . to-morrow."

"To-morrow," he echoed, and kissed her.

THE END

...ES HER WORLD GO ROUND

Faith Baldwin

—America's Most Enchanting Novelist—
Now Available in Warner Books Editions

—ALIMONY (75-235, 95¢)
—AND NEW STARS BURN (75-036, 95¢)
—ARIZONA STAR (78-897, $1.50)
—CAREER BY PROXY (75-755, 95¢)
—CHANGE OF HEART (65-807, 95¢)
—A CLOSE AND QUIET LOVE (75-650, 95¢)
—ENCHANTED OASIS (65-903, 95¢)
—GIVE LOVE THE AIR (75-014, 95¢)
—THE GOLDEN SHOESTRING (75-526, 95¢)
—THE HEART HAS WINGS (86-209, $1.25)
—THE HEART REMEMBERS (75-234, 95¢)
—HE MARRIED A DOCTOR (75-785, 95¢)
—THE INCREDIBLE YEAR (86-266, $1.25)

 A Warner Communications Company

- - - - - - - - - - - - - - - - - - - -

Please send me the books I have checked.

Enclose check or money order only, no cash please. Plus 35¢ per copy to cover postage and handling. N.Y. State residents add applicable sales tax.

Please allow 2 weeks for delivery.

WARNER BOOKS
P.O. Box 690
New York, N.Y. 10019

Name ....

Address ....

City .... State .... Zip ....

_____ Please send me your free mail order catalog